AUTUMN CUDDLES AND MUDDY PUDDLES

LITTLE BAMTON BOOK 4

BETH RAIN

Copyright © 2021 by Beth Rain

Autumn Cuddles and Muddy Puddles (Little Bamton Book 4)

First Publication: 27th August, 2021

All rights reserved.

No part of this book may be reproduced in any form or by any electronic or mechanical means, including information storage and retrieval systems. Except for use in any review, the reproduction or utilization of this work, in whole or in part, in any form by any electronic, mechanical or other means now known or hereafter invented, is forbidden without the written permission of the publisher.

Published by Beth Rain. The author may be contacted by email on bethrainauthor@gmail.com

❦ Created with Vellum

CHAPTER 1

'But I don't want you to gooooooo!' sobbed the little girl, grabbing a handful of Amber's checked shirt in her pudgy hands and burying her face in her thighs.

Amber felt her chest tighten. She would *not* cry - one sobbing five year old was bad enough.

'Come here,' she said, hoisting Belle up into her arms to give her a hug. 'I'm not going far, remember - I'm going to live in a princess castle, and you're going to help your mum and dad get the house ready for a new baby sister or brother!'

Amber cast a glance at Mia, Belle's mum, over the little girl's shoulder. Mia gave Amber an apologetic grimace as Belle wound her arms more tightly around Amber's neck. Clearly she wasn't about to get to load her last few boxes into Sue's truck without a fight.

'Cuppa?' chuckled Mia.

Amber nodded. 'I think that might be a plan!'

Mia King was Amber's live-in landlady - at least, she was for one more night. After three wonderful years lodging here in their family home, it was all change and, right now, Amber was pretty close to joining Belle in having a damn good cry. Instead, she was desperately trying to cling onto the practicalities of getting all her stuff moved out.

With her own car out of action at the garage, she'd borrowed Sue's truck for the job. Amber's aim was to get the rest of her boxes shifted today, have one more night's sleep in her nearly empty room, and then get everything sorted out in her new room at Bamton Hall in the morning.

Amber kicked the front door closed with her foot, leaving the last few boxes stacked in the hallway. They could wait for another twenty minutes. Sue had lent her the truck for the whole day while she was busy up at the allotments, so there was no rush.

Amber carried the little girl into the kitchen and plonked herself down onto one of the breakfast-bar stools with Belle on her lap - not that she had much choice in the matter as her sturdy little arms were still firmly wrapped around Amber's neck

'What's up?!' Amber grinned over at Richie, Belle's eleven-year-old brother, as Mia flicked the kettle on.

Richie shrugged. 'Maths homework.'

'Gross!' said Amber, earning herself one of his rare grins.

'You need help with her?' he said, nodding at his little sister.

'Nah, we're okay, aren't we Belly?' she said, ruffling the blond hair and earning herself a tearful giggle.

Amber couldn't believe that come tomorrow morning, this wasn't going to be her home anymore. She'd lived here for three years now, renting a room from Mia King and her husband Ben. It had started out as a convenient way to save a bit of cash - her small boxroom in the family home was relatively cheap for Little Bamton and had meant that she could afford to rent her unit in the craft centre as well.

When she'd moved in, she'd been planning on spending most of her time in her studio or out working. Her room had really just been somewhere handy to store her stuff and to pass out in at the end of the day. What she hadn't bargained on was becoming part of this chaotic little family.

Ben and Mia were about as tight-knit a couple as she'd ever met, and they'd become a weird mixture of best friends and surrogate parents to her - even though they were only a few years older than herself. And then, of course, there were the kids.

Amber had been practically allergic to the idea of children when she'd first moved in and hadn't envisioned spending any time with either of them. In fact, it had been her plan to just avoid them completely and pretend they didn't exist. Ha - fat chance!

It was lovely Richie who'd won her over first. He'd

been a gawky lad of eight, obsessed with her willow-weaving and full of questions about her projects and how everything worked. Even at eight, Richie had been a little old man, and Amber hadn't been able to resist the fact that he found everything about her fascinating.

Much to the delight of his parents, it hadn't been long before Richie'd begged to be allowed to go along on trips with Amber to scout for new willow suppliers - and he'd quickly become her sidekick at weekends too. He loved nothing more than spending a Saturday morning with Amber down at the craft centre, making his own little creations while she worked on her various commissions.

Even now that he'd progressed into a pre-teen, monosyllabic phase, Amber was still one of the few people who could actually get whole sentences out of the lad - something that she held as a badge of honour.

Then, of course, there was Belle - gorgeous, blond bundle of trouble that she was. It had taken Amber a bit longer to get used to the idea of hanging out with the troublesome toddler - but the little squirmer, with her sunny demeanour and cheeky grin, had been pretty determined.

Belle had the wonderful habit of appearing at the doorway of any room Amber happened to be in. Trundling in on clumsy, pudgy feet, she'd deliver soft toys, crayons and half-eaten rice-crackers into Amber's less than enthusiastic hands. It had been the constant demands for cuddles that had finally stolen Amber's heart.

So it was that the delighted Kings had found themselves not only with a lodger who'd become a part of the family - but a surrogate big sister mixed with cool aunty who just happened to be a willing and ready babysitter as well. They'd regularly joked that they should be paying her to live with them, not the other way around.

'You okay?' asked Mia, plonking Amber's favourite mug down on the breakfast bar in front of her with a gentle smile.

'Yeah, course,' said Amber, her voice coming out tight. What she really wanted to say was that she hated the idea of not living in the middle of this gorgeous family she now counted as her own. That she couldn't believe she was moving out just because she'd been offered a new job. But she couldn't because she didn't want to set Belle off again.

'You know, this job is going to be amazing for you,' said Mia, 'and you *do* get to live in a princess castle,' she laughed.

Amber nodded and managed to disentangle one arm from Belle so that she could sneak a sip of tea.

'Can we visit you in the castle?' said Belle, her voice muffled by Amber's jumper.

'Of course! Loads!' said Amber.

'And Richie too?'

'Definitely. Richie's coming up to help me, aren't you mate?'

Richie nodded, not looking up from his exercise book.

'Bamton Hall's only just up the road,' said Mia, 'and Amber said maybe you can go for a sleepover one day when she's settled in!'

'A princess sleepover?'

Amber widened her eyes in horror at Mia, but it was too late - the idea had already been planted.

'Yes - a princess sleepover,' chuckled Mia, then stuck her tongue out at Amber as Belle cheered and finally lifted her face out of Amber's jumper.

Ah crap, a princess sleepover?! Even in her late twenties, Amber was such a tom-boy that the idea of a *princess* sleepover filled her with horror - but she'd do anything for this little miss, as Mia very well knew.

Amber had absolutely dreaded having to tell Mia and Ben that she'd accepted Horace's offer of a job up at Bamton Hall for the winter. She knew her friends would be happy for her, but the job came with a room in the house itself. It was a bit of a dream come true - but it meant leaving the warmth and comfort of family life with the Kings behind her. And she had to admit, it broke her heart in a way she hadn't been expecting.

What Amber really hadn't anticipated was the sheer relief on her friends' faces when she'd broken the news to them one night after the kids were in bed. After having a good laugh at Amber's reaction, Ben gently explained that Mia was pregnant with kiddie number three, and no matter how they'd tried to figure a way around it, there was no escaping the fact that they'd need Amber's room for their growing brood.

'So, what's the plan for the rest of the day?' asked Mia, placing a cup of juice down next to Belle as she finally hopped across to her own stool.

'I've got my last load of boxes to drop up to the hall while I've still got Sue's truck. Then I'm going to drop it back down to the village, leave it in the pub car park and wander over to Dragonfly Cottage - we've got book club tonight at Emmy's, so I'll be back late. Then tomorrow, I'm off up to the hall, and you can get the paintbrushes out and start turning my room into a nursery!'

'Yay!' squealed Belle. 'I'm going to help. I'm good at painting.'

'Oh . . . goodie,' deadpanned Mia, making Amber chuckle.

'So wait, let me get this straight,' said Emmy, carefully placing the tray of drinks down on her potting table in the conservatory of Dragonfly Cottage and handing the glasses around to the others. 'You - *Miss Amber "I can't stand children" Reid* - are heartbroken because you're about to move out of the most hectic house in the whole of Little Bamton?'

Amber grinned and nodded. 'Yup - who'd have thought it, eh?!'

'Well, I think it's sweet,' said Caro. 'Anyway - you could always think about having a baby of your own!'

This made Amber laugh so hard that she sprayed the sip of champagne she'd just taken right down her chin. 'No. Thanks. Really!' she laughed. 'I think I'll get over it. In fact - it's a miracle - I already am!' she gave a little shudder. 'And anyway - we'd have to be talking immaculate conception all the way, here!'

'Well, you could start dating . . .' said Caro.

'I'm quite happy as I am, thanks!' said Amber.

'But-'

'And waaaay too busy,' she added, cutting her friend off before she could go any further. 'This project is going to be full-on.'

Caro gave a little shrug. 'Thanks Em,' she said, taking a glass of elderflower fizz.

'You sure you don't want champagne too?' asked Emmy, waggling the remainder of the bottle at Caro.

Caro shook her head. 'Nah, thanks. I'm good.'

'More for the rest of us,' laughed Lucy, reaching over and taking her own glass from Emmy.

'I'm gutted Eve isn't back yet,' said Sue. 'Feels like the whole group should be here to celebrate your move, Amber.'

Amber shrugged. 'She'll be back soon - then we can have another get-together. We can do the whole "ladies who lunch" thing up at the hall. And anyway, it's so cool Eve's busy hanging her own exhibition in the big smoke. Just think - all those gorgeous pieces of our little village on show up in London.'

'Still, feels like a lot is changing, doesn't it?' said Sue with a sigh. 'Eve and Finn hopping between here and London, you moving up to Bamton Hall, Jon finally moving in here with Emmy, and . . . and other stuff too,' she finished, looking a bit awkward.

Amber raised her eyebrows at Sue. 'It's all good change though, isn't it? At least, I hope it is!'

'Of course it is!' said Lucy, grabbing Sue's hand and giving it a squeeze. 'Cheers,' she added, raising her glass as Emmy threw herself into the corner of the second sofa next to Caro. 'Here's to Amber's new job and posh digs!'

Amber raised her glass and took a gulp, trying to swallow down the lump of emotion that seemed to have been lodged in her throat all day.

'It *is* going to be quite a change for you, going from living in that small house with the kids and Ben and Mia to rattling around Bamton Hall with just Horace for company,' said Caro, swirling her elderflower fizz thoughtfully.

'I'm not even going to have Horace for company to start with,' laughed Amber, hoping Caro wasn't going to start in on *babies* and *dating* again. 'Don't forget - he and Violet are off on their romantic few days in France first thing in the morning - and I'll be dog-sitting Diesel and Tarmac.'

'Poor you!' chuckled Emmy.

'I love those dogs,' said Sue.

'Me too,' nodded Amber, grinning at the thought of the smiling faces and permanently wagging tails of Horace's pair of chocolate labs.

Dog-sitting was definitely one of the perks of her new job as far as Amber was concerned, and she'd gladly agreed when Horace practically begged her to do it.

'Well, you're not going to be up there all on your own, are you?' said Sue. 'Horace's new Estate Manager's due to move in any time now - or at least, that's what Alf told me the other day when we were up at the allotments.'

'Ooh yes . . .' said Emmy. 'The mysterious William Jones. Does anyone know anything about him?'

'Nope,' laughed Lucy. 'But no doubt the poor man will be the talk of Little Bamton the minute he arrives!'

'So true,' chuckled Emmy.

'It's bizarre though, don't you think?!' said Sue. 'Horace has lived so quietly up at the hall for so long - joining in with stuff in the village and letting locals potter around the gardens up there. He's always seemed happy to trundle along - and now it's like he's on some kind of mission . . . I don't know what's gotten into him!'

'I do,' said Amber. 'Violet!'

'Ah, good point,' said Sue.

'She's like a human cattle-prod, that woman,' said

Emmy. 'Let's face it - she's the one who, erm, *encouraged* me to finally ask Jon to move in here with me.'

'Well, good thing too,' said Caro, 'and it's lovely to see her and Horace having such a good time together. If you think about it, it's all down to Eve, really. That art workshop was just what the pair of them needed to throw them together at last.'

'Right!' said Amber. 'And thanks to that, I now have an entire paddock up at Bamton Hall to grow my own willow!'

'Look at you,' laughed Lucy, 'he's given you a large, muddy puddle to play in and you're as happy as Larry.'

Amber laughed. 'A pig in muck - that's what my mum said! But it's a dream come true. I get somewhere to live while I'm working, and an acre to grow my own willow, and in return, Horace gets a live-in dog sitter, a whole bunch of willowy-goodness and . . .'

'And?' prompted Emmy with a twinkle in her eye.

'You know I'm not allowed to tell you until he announces it!' laughed Amber.

'Damn,' grinned Emmy. 'So close!'

CHAPTER 2

*A*mber stuck out her hand and indicated before swinging her bike between the imposing pillars that marked the entrance to Bamton Hall. She let out a huge sigh. The ride up from the village had proved way more knackering than usual, but the sight of this grand sweep of drive underneath the golden leaves of the beech trees made the whole thing worth it. Almost.

Why she'd thought going to a book club meeting the night before moving day was a good idea was anyone's guess! Her head was pounding and the post-champagne samba band in her skull was in full swing. It hadn't helped that she'd cried buckets after waving goodbye to the kids - a fact that she'd be carefully keeping quiet about next time she saw Caro.

It wasn't that she had *completely* ruled out the family thing, or that she *never* wanted to find love - but she was perfectly happy with her life exactly how it was right now, thanks all the same! She loved her work, loved her friends, and loved Little Bamton. Why would she risk all that by hunting for something - or *someone* - she didn't actively need or want in her life?!

Amber sighed again. That train of thought was definitely *way* too heavy for her sore head to handle. She rubbed her face roughly with her sleeve. She knew she probably looked a right state - but luckily there wasn't going to be anyone at the hall to see her hangover in action. Horace and Violet should be well on their way to France by now, and this new Will bloke wasn't due to start for at least a week.

The massive old spare key Horace had handed her the day before was safely zipped in her jacket pocket, and her new home awaited. She'd get the chance to play *lady of the manor* to her heart's content for a few days with just the dogs for company - and frankly, she couldn't imagine anything more perfect.

Amber loved her friends dearly, but she also loved being on her own. There was nothing better than tromping around outside and doing her thing - which mostly consisted of planting, tending or making things out of willow. She had always been happy in her own company. It wasn't that she didn't enjoy being with others, it was just that she didn't need their presence to feel completely content and at ease.

Pausing for a moment to give her legs a rest, Amber gulped in the cool morning air. The day had a crisp tang to it, scented by golden leaves and damp earth. It held that strange sense of possibility that always arrived with autumn - and it made her skin tingle. This move meant a lot of change, but not all change had to be bad, did it?

She twisted in the saddle to check that the little cardboard box of belongings was still safely tied to the bike behind her. She was so grateful that Sue had lent her the truck the previous day and that she'd managed to get all her heavy stuff moved already. All she had with her now was this box containing a few essential last minute bits and pieces, and her rucksack with the last of her bedding and a change of clothes - plus the precious box of cookies Mia and Belle had baked for her.

There was no doubt about it, the sooner she got her little old Ford back from the garage, the better. She was lost without it. As much as she enjoyed cycling, her bike wouldn't exactly be any good when it came to moving weaving supplies around. Piling cuttings and withies into the back of the Ford was always difficult enough - but the idea of trying to strap them to the bike somehow was laughable.

Horace had already said that she was welcome to borrow the estate's old Land Rover if she needed it, and by the way the guys at the garage had sucked their teeth when she'd pulled in with the Ford belching steam from under its bonnet, she had a sneaking suspicion she'd be taking him up on the offer.

She wasn't going to be worrying about that today, though. Today was all about settling into her new home - and what a home it was. As Amber kicked off and started to pedal again, crunching along the manicured gravel drive, Bamton Hall came into view. She couldn't believe that she'd be living here!

Of course, she'd seen it hundreds of times before, but as she gazed at the golden stone glowing in the soft autumn light, her heart leapt in excitement - her new home had turrets, for heaven's sake! Amber let out a little squeal despite her hangover and couldn't stop a huge grin from spreading across her face. This was going to be amazing.

Pulling up in front of the house at last, Amber hopped off the bike and leant it gently against the wall. The rusty old thing was *definitely* not posh enough to be on show next to her new home, but right now she was too excited to head inside and check out her room again to worry about it - she'd find somewhere more permanent to stash it out of the way later. Besides, the hall was currently closed to all visitors, so it wasn't like it was going to be in anyone's way.

She made her way around the side of the building, the cardboard box under one arm and her rucksack slung over one shoulder. Horace had said that he would shut the dogs in his library before he and Violet set off - supposedly they were as good as gold when they were in there. In theory, they'd had a long walk first thing, but still - Amber wanted to make sure they got another one as soon as possible. She'd quickly drop her things off in her new room and then head down to let them out for a zoom around.

Given that the mischievous chocolate labs were lovingly known as the "terrible two" by everyone in the village, Amber had breathed a sigh of relief to find that there was at least one room in the house that was dog-proofed and safe to leave them in if she ever needed to. Horace had also advised her that they slept in there, and on her head be it if she decided to try any kind of foolhardy experiment like having them sleep in her room with her. The words "slippers" and "chew toy" had featured quite heavily in that warning.

Unlocking the heavy wooden side door with the ridiculously old, oversized key from her pocket, Amber let herself into the hallway and paused to listen. Bamton Hall might currently be devoid of any human inhabitants, but it was far from silent. The gentle ticking of the long-case clock sounded warm and inviting and seemed to be having a chat with the house itself as the breeze outside drew gentle rattles and creaks from the windows and woodwork. The whole place exuded friendliness, and instead of feeling like an interloper, Amber felt like the old house was inviting her in.

She padded down the hallway, her footsteps making no sound on the long strip of worn, patterned rug that covered the wooden floorboards. She'd take her things upstairs, have a quick peep at her room again, and then head straight back down to the library.

Trailing her hand along the sweep of the wooden handrail as she navigated the stairs, Amber breathed in the scent of beeswax polish and lavender. She revelled in a golden beam of sunlight that shone through a leaded window on the landing above her, illuminating the dust-motes dancing in the fragrant air. This was home. She couldn't believe it - *this* was home.

Horace had given her the choice of three different bedrooms when she'd accepted the job, and Amber had taken this one in the West Wing - much to Horace's surprise. It wasn't the largest, nor the one with the "best" view - but she'd fallen in love with it on sight. She'd seen it on a grey, drizzly day, and yet the room had felt like it was filled with sunshine because of the primrose yellow, silk wallpaper.

Pushing the door open now, Amber stepped in and smiled. Although she hadn't had time yesterday to unpack all her things, just the fact that they were here was a huge comfort. It wouldn't take her long and this little corner of Bamton Hall would feel like it had always belonged to her.

Placing the box down on the bed and then shrugging the backpack off her shoulders, she dumped it unceremoniously onto a large armchair and made her way over to stare out of the deep-set window, sinking onto the window-seat for just a moment or two.

This view was the other reason she'd fallen in love

with the room. Rather than overlooking the main gardens, her bedroom looked out across the wilder parts of Bamton Hall's grounds. From here, she could just about make out her own patch of heaven - the little paddock that would soon be host to a range of specialist willow. Amber used far too much willow each year to contemplate growing enough for her work. Luckily, she had several suppliers she could rely on for the basics, but she'd been dying to grow some of the more specialist varieties she wanted to try out - and this was the perfect opportunity.

The girls might have called it a muddy puddle last night, but this was Amber's dream - and she couldn't believe that Horace had made it come true. Sure, it *was* muddy - the old clay drainage system had given up the ghost having been neglected for far too long, so the field was boggy - but that was just how willow liked it! Give it a couple of years and she'd have the bed established, they'd dry out the ground and stop the neighbouring fields from flooding - as well as providing a bit of a windbreak.

Of course, Amber wouldn't be living here that long. She was here for the winter - just long enough to bring Horace's vision of a sculpture trail around the grounds to life. The idea of having to move out brought a lump to her throat.

'Don't be an idiot!' she muttered, giving herself a little shake. She had the whole winter to enjoy being a tenant of Bamton Hall. She had her paddock to populate and Horace's grand plans to work on. It really was the dream commission - sure, she wasn't exactly getting paid her normal rate (or anything much at all, if she was being honest), but she was being provided with board, lodgings and land.

Plus, she was so excited to be a part of Bamton Hall opening its doors to the wider world - and she hoped that her work would help Horace attract some new visitors.

It was a bit early in the season to start planting her new willow bed yet though, so instead, she'd be getting everything ready to start work on the sculptures first.

Not today, though. Today was about unpacking and settling in. And before she even started on that, she had two furry bulldozers downstairs who would, no doubt, be gagging for a walk by now.

She grabbed a checked, padded jacket to pull on against the tickly autumn breeze and then, with one last loving glance at her sunshine-filled haven, pulled the door closed behind her and made her way back downstairs.

When he'd shown her around the hall, Horace had told her that she'd have the West Wing bathroom all to herself. He'd been so apologetic about the lack of ensuite it had made her laugh. After sharing the tiny bathroom at the King's with the entire family, not much could phase her. Frankly, being able to have a bath without a little hand knocking insistently at the door the entire time would be a novelty!

She also had full use of the hall's massive kitchen, and Amber had breathed a sigh of relief when she'd spotted a microwave tucked away in the corner. She didn't much fancy having to stoke up the old wood-fired range every time she fancied heating up some soup! Then there was the visitor's lounge that she'd be sharing with this Will bloke. It was situated right between the two wings and was a lovely room that managed to be cosy despite its size. It boasted a huge open fireplace and plenty of sturdy wooden furniture that had been polished to a rosy glow over the years.

As soon as she was back downstairs, Amber let out a laugh. So much for Tarmac and Diesel patiently awaiting a walk - she could hear the two little so-and-sos from here. Scratching, whining and frustrated little woofs emanated from the other side of library's panelled door.

Bracing herself for a furry typhoon, Amber turned the handle and was promptly engulfed in enough doggy cuddles and slobber to last a lifetime. It was like someone had attached springs to their feet, and she laughed as her whole vision was filled for a moment with blurred chocolate coloured fur.

'Down, you nutters!' she giggled, trying to both pat them and push them away from her at the same time so that she could actually greet them properly. 'Come on, come on, get back a sec,' she laughed.

She really needed to grab their leads, which Horace had promised to leave on the library desk, otherwise she wouldn't have bothered trying to fight her way past.

'Oh my goodness,' gasped Amber, finally catching sight of the room beyond the doorway as the two dogs did a kind of waggy victory-lap around the library. 'What have you *done?!*'

CHAPTER 3

The library had been torn apart. The leather sofa looked like roadkill with its white, fluffy stuffing spilling out over the carpet. The open fireplace looked like it had received their loving attention too. One of the hell-hounds had clearly decided to have a good dig in the bank of cold ash left over from a long-extinguished fire, and there was a halo of soot and ash that extended out into the room by at least six feet in all directions. The grey-black paw-prints that lead away from this were sprinkled liberally throughout the entire room.

The desk chair had been overturned. Amber moved towards it in a horrified kind of trance, meaning to set it back in its proper place, but she came to a halt when she noticed there were paw prints across the green leather desktop and the writing paper left there too.

'You two are in soooo much trouble!' she breathed.

She turned and was met with two grinning faces and a pair of madly wagging tails. Diesel and Tarmac had both plonked their behinds down on the flagstones in front of the fire and were watching her every move.

'Look at you - acting like butter wouldn't melt!' she said, hoiking the chair up off the floor.

She'd need to clear this mess up, and there was no getting away from the fact that she was going to have to call Horace. It wasn't as though she'd be able to replace the decimated sofa before he got home.

Still - first things first - perhaps it would be better to take the terrible two out for a jaunt straight away. If she managed to get them properly tired out, perhaps they'd have a doze when they got back, giving her a bit of peace and quiet to sort this out.

Reaching for the two rope leads, she spotted the bag of treats Horace had promised to leave for her, along with an envelope with her name on it.

'Right. Really not a good start,' she said, picking up the treat bag, turning it on end and shaking it. Two lonely treats fell onto the desk.

Both sets of furry chocolate ears lifted in response and Amber rolled her eyes. 'Bit late for that, you little thieves!' she said. 'Besides, I reckon you've had enough of these . . . or at least, one of you has!' It was clear that whoever belonged to the sooty pawprints now adorning the desktop had also snaffled an entire week's stash of treats while he'd been up there. She'd have to get some more in, otherwise she suspected she might have a mutiny on her hands. Amber grabbed the envelope and popped it into her pocket. She'd check it out once she'd got this pair safely outside.

'Right, chaos hounds!' she said, heading over to them and clipping a lead to each of their collars. 'Let's get out of here.' Horace had said that there was no need for leads unless there were members of the public around, but frankly, she wasn't keen on the idea of the dogs rampaging through the hall and doing any more damage.

She needn't have worried. The leads seemed to work like a magic charm on the furballs, and they trotted alongside her like model citizens as they made their way to the side door, tails wagging in tandem, clearly happy now that they knew a walk was in the offing.

As soon as she was back out in the fresh air, Amber breathed a sigh of relief. She'd thought dog sitting for a few days would be a soothing kind of therapy, but somehow she was getting the feeling that this might not be entirely accurate. Never mind. At least the state of the library meant that the dogs really couldn't do much more damage in there on her watch - it was already completely trashed.

Now that they were safely out of reach of any expensive furniture or breakable antiques, Amber unclipped their leads and laughed as she watched the dogs zoom in wide circles around her, tongues lolling and tails blurring.

She set off in the direction of her paddock . . . she couldn't resist a quick look at her new kingdom. Draping the leads around her neck to keep them safe, Amber briefly lifted her face towards the soft golden sunshine, letting it kiss her skin. Being up here for the whole winter was going to be bliss.

She thrust her hands into her checked shirt pockets and felt the crumple of paper. Of course - the note from Horace.

Giving a sharp whistle so that the dogs followed in her general direction, Amber slit open the thick cream envelope with its sooty, doggy paw print on the front.

Dear Amber,

Welcome home, dear girl! I'm so sorry not to be able to be here to greet you - but I hope you make yourself at home while I'm away. Thanks again for looking after my boys.

Violet has stocked the fridge up with some basics, and check in the pantry too - she's made sure there are plenty of treats. Help yourself to any DVDs, books or music that takes your fancy in the Library (you'll find that the internet and phone signal are patchy up here at best, so good luck with Netflix!)

Speaking of the library - the boys did a number on the sofa in there last night. It's a shame - third one they've eaten this year. I didn't get the chance to tidy it up this morning, but don't worry too much about it - they'll only rip out more stuffing until the whole thing's moved out of there.

I'm sure you've already found them, but I've left an almost full packet of treats on the desk - no more than four a day and don't let them trick you - those pleading eyes are powerful!

Oh - I should mention that Will may decide to come down a day or two earlier than he originally anticipated. His room and office in the East Wing are all ready for him - so nothing for you to do there. I just wanted to let you know in case he appears before I get back. He's a good lad, and I hope you both hit it off. Bit of a tough time recently, so hopefully the magic of Little Bamton will work its wonders on him.

We're both sending love, and thanks, and look forward to working together on all our exciting plans when we get back.

Oh - the Landy is in the shed next to the gardener's hut. All fuelled up and keys are in there if you need them.

Give the boys a kiss from me and tell them I'm missing them already.

Yours Faithfully,
Horace x

Amber looked over at the dogs who were gleefully rolling in something that she'd rather not think about. Maybe she wouldn't pass that kiss from their dad on *right* now.

'Oi, you two!' she called, patting her thighs.

With much wriggling, both Tarmac and Diesel hoiked themselves to their feet and dashed back over towards her.

'Your dad sends his love but . . . EEW! What's that?!'

Their glossy chocolate backs were smeared with something that was wafting a pretty horrific stink in her direction.

'Really?! Only you two could manage to find badger poop on our first walk together. Fine. Your dad sends his love and a kiss - but you're not getting one of those smelling like that. Come on, change of plan!'

With a sigh, Amber turned on her heel and changed direction. She'd take them down to the little stream that ran through the bottom of Bamton Hall's gardens. Time for a quick wash for these two before they went anywhere near the house again.

It didn't take much convincing to get them both into the chilly water, and they threw themselves into one of the deeper pools with enthusiasm. Amber knew that it wouldn't help much and that she'd probably need to get a bucket of water on the pair of them before they went back into the house, but maybe it would rinse some of the worst of the poop off their sides. Besides, if nothing else, they seemed to be enjoying themselves.

Squatting down, she plonked her behind on one of the large, round boulders at the edge of the stream and watched the dogs playing in the water. There were definitely worse ways to spend a Sunday morning in October, and the fresh air was already working wonders on her head.

Saying that, there was still something niggling away

in the back of her mind - an unspoken worry getting in the way of her truly enjoying herself. It was that throwaway mention in Horace's letter - the vague possibility that Will might turn up earlier than expected. Damn. That would certainly put a dampener on her nice peaceful few days to herself!

Still, maybe it wouldn't be so bad if it did happen. It would give them a chance to get to know each other - they'd have to work together at some point after all.

As Horace's new Estate Manager, Will was here to get the place in a better shape. The boundaries, fences, trees and pathways all needed attention - but first there needed to be a plan of action and someone to manage the whole process, otherwise it was going to turn into a massively expensive free-for-all - and that was where Will came in.

From what Horace had already told her, it sounded like Will had some experience in managing large projects, but he hadn't really gone into the details. Or - *maybe* he had. If she was being completely honest, she hadn't really been listening that closely - she'd been too busy eyeballing her new mud patch.

Well, if he did turn up early, she'd just have to deal with it. Still, she'd much prefer it if he didn't - she wasn't brilliant at making nice with strangers. Her mum always said it was because she was such a tomboy and that her manners needed a bit of polishing, but Amber didn't agree. She just couldn't see the point of pretending to be anyone but herself - and for some reason, that seemed to upset some people. Sod it. She wasn't going to worry about that right now.

Amber struggled to her feet. It was time for some tea and toast now that the fresh autumn air had blown away the majority of her hangover and the river had washed away most of the poop from the dogs.

'Come on, you blighters!' she called, clicking her fingers.

The boys had been busy dunking each other under the water with their front paws. On hearing her voice, they paused, cocked their heads for a second, and then carried on as if nothing had happened.

'Tarmac! Diesel! Here!' she said, trying to keep a straight face.

This time they listened and sloshed their way up the bank towards her. Huh. She should have thought this through a bit more carefully. Both dogs came right up to her feet and then went into dual, full-body shakes, spraying her with a delightful mixture of river water and diluted poop droplets.

'You little buggers!' she squealed, raising the back of her hand to wipe the unholy soup off her face. Great - now it wasn't just the dogs that were going to need a shower! 'Come on. Let's go!' she scrambled up the bank and the dogs followed, gambolling around her like lunatics as they headed for the back door of the hall again.

Amber slowed, wondering how best to navigate this bit. She couldn't let them inside like this - but she couldn't leave them on their own out here while she went in search of a bucket of water and some old towels either. She paused next to the closed door, thinking hard. Maybe they'd just dry off in the sunshine and the whole poop situation wouldn't be quite so bad then? Fat chance! She'd just have to take them inside and straight up to her bathroom. Maybe she could get them both into the shower somehow.

Amber was just reaching for the leads around her neck when the door opened from inside, making her shriek and jump back in surprise. She had just enough time to register an equally shocked, slightly bristly face before two stinky chocolate blurs flew straight past her and completely poleaxed the stranger. Whoever it was disappeared under a wriggling mass of overexcited Labrador as the boys treated him to a very soggy, smelly welcome.

CHAPTER 4

Amber was caught between utter horror and the desire to giggle as she watched the figure on the ground wrestling with both Diesel and Tarmac at once. The dogs had clearly decided that this was the best game ever invented. Amber had a sneaking suspicion that their new playmate felt quite the opposite, given the angry, grunting sounds coming from him as he did his utmost to avoid engaging in double doggy snogs.

Suddenly realising that perhaps she should be doing a bit more to help him rather than standing there, staring at the disaster as it unfolded in front of her, Amber hurried forward and grabbed the dogs by their collars. Quickly pulling them off the poor guy, she clipped their leads on and towed them away to a safe distance to give him the chance to get his bearings.

'Are you okay?' she asked, watching as he scrambled

off the floor using the door frame as support to hoist himself up.

'Erm . . . I think so?' he said, brushing down what had probably been a very smart pair of chinos. They now resembled a dishrag with legs. He raked his fingers through his tufty, sandy coloured hair. 'God, *what's* that awful smell?' he asked, sniffing the arm of his jacket and then recoiling.

'Badger poop,' she muttered. 'Courtesy of these two.' She watched as the guy turned an interesting shade of green and quickly stripped the jacket off.

'Sorry to ask but - who are you?' said Amber. Man, how awkward could she get? But she needed to check who else was ambling around the hall without her knowledge.

'Will Jones. New Estate Manager,' he said, going to hold out his hand for her to shake, then dropping it quickly with an awkward jerk, probably realising that a) it was covered in badger poo and b) both Amber's hands were occupied in trying to keep the dogs in check. Diesel and Tarmac were still both straining towards him, clearly keen for another round of snog-the-new-boy.

'I'm guessing you're Amber?' he said raising his eyebrows at her.

'Yeah. Blimey, you're here early!'

She watched with interest as Will shrugged and scuffed one foot against the ground. 'Well, thought I'd get an early start on things. Can be easier to get the lay of the land without the owner around sometimes, so I thought I'd make the most of it.'

Amber looked at him in surprise. She'd thought that he was meant to be a friend of Horace's family somehow - his best friend's son or something like that. It wasn't exactly the friendliest comment he could make, was it?!

'Oh. Right,' she said. There, that was safe. She didn't want to put the guy's nose out of joint after he'd just been soaked by the terrible two. After all, he'd been put on the spot as much as she had. Maybe she should cut him a bit of slack. 'Look - I'm really sorry about these two. I had no idea anyone else was around.'

'Well, it's clear they're going to have to be one of the first changes Horace makes when he opens to the public again. Can't have those two running around if they're not trained.'

'You can't ask him to get rid of the dogs!' breathed Amber in a low voice, not wanting to hurt Diesel and Tarmac's feelings.

'I didn't say *get rid of.* But Horace wants me to tell him how things should work - what needs to be introduced - and what should go. That's what I'm here to do,' came the stiff reply. 'He's got lots of ideas, and not all of them are going to stick. Now, if you'll excuse me, I think I'd better go shower and change.'

'Yeah. Okay,' said Amber, doing her best to mask the fact that her hackles were already up after this short and not so sweet interaction. 'I've got to clean these two up and sort out the library anyway.'

'I saw. I'm taking it that was the dogs too?'

'Well it wasn't me!' she snapped.

'I'll have to talk to Horace. That sofa-'

'Don't bother. He already knows. Look, I'll catch you later, okay? The smell's starting to make me feel sick!'

Amber tugged on the dogs' leads and wandered away with them towards the back of the house. She cast a quick glance over her shoulder before rounding the corner, but Will had already disappeared back inside.

Crap. That definitely hadn't been the ideal first encounter. She'd hoped that they'd get along, considering that they'd be working together for the next few months, but there had just been something about him that had rubbed her up the wrong way. Sure, the boys were trouble, but this was their home and they were Horace's family!

Family that, right now, no matter how much she wanted to stick up for them, smelled like the wrong end of a badger and were causing her a bit of a conundrum. She couldn't exactly take them up to her bathroom now that she knew Mr High and Mighty was in the house, could she?

Wandering aimlessly towards the gardener's hut, Amber nearly uttered a prayer of thanks when she spotted an outdoor tap with a reel of hose at its side.

Ideal! She'd hose the boys down properly. Now, if only there was something in one of these sheds that she could use as a makeshift towel, she'd be sorted.

Quickly tying the leads to the stand-pipe, leaving the dogs snuffling around in the long grass at its base, she let herself into the gardener's hut first. Surely there must be something in here she could use! But no - a pile of deck chairs, an old, galvanised watering can and several stacks of seed trays weren't going to get her very far. Balls.

She quickly made her way around the back and stuck her head into the other shed, which only held the old Landy and a bench full of tools. Amber peered into the front of the cab, but it was empty. Hell, if she couldn't find anything, she would just have to hose the boys down and let them shake it off as best as they could before sorting them out back in the library.

As a last resort, she yanked open the back door of the Landy. Jackpot! There was an old, moth-eaten purple sweatshirt lying on one of the benches. That would do better than nothing - and she could always pop it in the washing machine when they were finished.

'Okay boys,' she said, heading back outside and turning the tap on so that the hose sprang to life, 'time to de-badger!'

∼

'Done!' said Amber, tying the top of the black bin liner full of sofa-stuffing and peering around her to check for anything else that the dogs could conceivably eat, decimate or destroy. 'Now, will you two promise to behave while I go and figure out what the deal with the new boy is?'

Two pairs of melting chocolate eyes watched her from the giant, fluffy dog bed under the grand mullion windows of the library as if to say "*Us? Trouble?*"

Amber couldn't help but smile at them. She grabbed the two remaining treats from the desk and gave them one each. 'Good lads.'

They definitely weren't, but frankly, she had a feeling that the image of William Jones getting thoroughly Labradored might be the one thing that kept her going - especially if he turned out to be half as bad as she suspected.

Tired out from their exploits, the dogs snaffled their treats and promptly flumped down on their bed like two giant bookends. As it turned out, they'd thoroughly enjoyed being hosed down - giving Amber the sneaking suspicion that it might be something that happened on a semi-regular basis. They certainly seemed to treat it as a huge game - which was fine with her, considering that it was a game that made them smell a whole lot better, even if it left her drenched to the skin.

'Okay, behave,' she said, giving each of them a final pat. She grabbed the bin bag and the sodden sweatshirt, let herself out of the library and carefully shut the door behind her.

'Time for my own shower,' she muttered, dumping the bag and the sweatshirt on the hallway floor. She'd collect them later on her way back down to the kitchen. Amber bounded up the stairs towards her bathroom.

Ten minutes later, she felt a whole lot better. She was even feeling a bit bad for Will. He hadn't asked to be floored by those two nutters, had he? It was no wonder that he'd been a bit less than charitable towards them. Amber decided to get dressed and go downstairs to find him so that she could make a second attempt at an introduction - hopefully a slightly more civilised one this time.

Amber was just towelling her short blond crop when her mobile rang. She checked the screen to find Horace's number flashing up.

'Hey boss!' she answered with a grin. 'How's France?'

'We've reached Brittany and it's beautiful!'

'Brilliant.'

'I just wanted to check on my boys,' he said, sounding slightly sheepish.

'Oh, they're . . . fine!' she said, not sure how much to share with him. After all, she didn't want him worrying.

'You hesitated. What's up?'

'Nothing - they really are fine!' said Amber quickly.

'But-?'

'But they dug in the fireplace in the library, spread soot everywhere, got up on your desk, ate all the treats, rolled in badger poo, flattened Will and then had to have a shower before I could let them back into the house.'

'So - about standard for a morning at Bamton Hall then!' boomed Horace with a laugh.

Amber couldn't help but grin. She *knew* he hadn't told her everything when he'd begged her to dog sit!

'Did you find their towels?' he asked.

'Towels?'

'Sure - I keep them hanging up on the pegs in the back porch.'

Of course he did!

'No - sorry - I'm afraid I used an old sweatshirt out of the Land Rover. Don't worry, I'll wash it and put it back!'

Horace laughed again. 'Not to worry - that one's Alf's - I think it's been in there for about a year now!'

'Cool. Okay. Anyway - I've sorted the library out a bit.'

'Thanks Amber. Don't be surprised if it's right back to square one tomorrow morning though. Hang on a minute - did you say something about the boys flattening Will?!'

'Yup. That was his warm welcome to his new job. Knocked off his feet and then treated to plenty of doggy kisses and badger poo.'

'Oh dear,' sighed Horace.

'Too right, I don't think he was very impressed with them.'

'They'll learn to love each other,' said Horace.

Amber stayed quiet. She wasn't so sure.

'Look - it's probably a good thing he's turned up so early - gives the pair of you a chance to get to know each other without us two old fogeys cramping your style.'

'Watch who you're calling an old fogey!'

'Hi Violet!' Amber laughed as her voice cut across Horace's. 'Look, I don't think Will's too happy with me either for some reason - I should probably have had the boys on their leads. Don't worry though, I'll go and make up with him in a bit.'

'Good, good. That would be good,' said Horace, sounding rather distracted. 'I mean to say, he *is* going to be your manager, so it would probably be a good thing for you to be on good terms from the start.'

'My ... wait, my manager?!' said Amber.

'Of course. Much better than me. I've got no clue about these things. Anyway, give the boys a kiss from me - don't let them give you any trouble. I've got to go - we're off to find our first hotel. There's dancing this evening! Toodleoo.'

Before she could say another word, Horace had disappeared.

Shit. Manager? She hadn't been expecting that. Not so much that it was this Will bloke, but more that she hadn't been expecting to have a manager at all, if she was honest. She'd thought that after her discussions with Horace the deal was done, the broad plans agreed, and all she had to do was get on with the work and make it all happen.

What if Will decided that she was one of the "ideas that needed to go." No. She couldn't let that happen. Not only was this her dream project, but it was also perfect for Bamton Hall. The sculptures would be an attraction that would be a huge talking point and bring in new visitors, and her willow bed would have a beneficial impact on the estate grounds as a whole - not to mention the biodiversity side of things.

Horace was right. It was time to make nice and try for a better second impression with Will, otherwise things could get really rather uncomfortable around here.

CHAPTER 5

Deciding that making nice with Will was more of a priority than blow-drying her hair, Amber simply ran her fingers through her short crop and headed out in search of him. She'd only gone about ten paces along the landing when she quickly turned and let herself back into her room.

Rummaging in her rucksack, she drew out the box of cookies that Mia and Belle had given her. Perfect - no one could resist a cup of tea and a chocolate chip cookie, could they?

She hurried down to their sitting room first, but he was nowhere to be seen. Damn. It would be typical if he'd decided to head out onto the estate already. Now that she'd decided a truce was in order, she needed to sort it out straight away. It was just the way she was. Her mum had always said she was a bit of a bulldozer. Her dad just said she was determined. Either way, it wasn't surprising that she had an affinity with the terrible two who were probably busy with their second round of library decimation right now!

Right, nothing for it but to try the kitchen. If Will wasn't there, then she'd just have to make herself a cup of tea and set to work on the cookies single-handedly.

She made her way downstairs to the huge, slate-floored room, and pushed the door open.

'Hey!' said Will, looking over from one of the worktops.

'Oh, erm - hi!' she said.

She could kick herself. The minute she spotted him, her hand went up to her damp hair of its own accord and started twiddling with it. What *was* she, a teenager?

'Can I get you a coffee?' he asked, looking slightly awkward. 'I'm guessing you probably need it after sorting the dogs out?'

Amber smiled at him. 'Please, that'd be great.'

'Okay. I brought my machine with me. What do you fancy?' he said, rattling a box of those expensive metal pods at her.

'Fancy!' laughed Amber. 'Do you have just coffee-coffee? With all the caff?'

'Sure,' he said, selecting one and placing it into the machine.

'Thanks. I brought cookies!'

Will pressed a button on the machine and it sprang to life. Amber was glad of the loud graunching sounds - at least it gave her a minute to collect herself. Crikey -

she'd only been a tenant of Bamton Hall for a morning, and she was already getting ready to reach for the smelling salts.

She popped the cookies down on the scrubbed pine table in the centre of the room and did her best not to ogle the decidedly pert bum in front of her as Will frothed milk for her coffee. Yum! How had she not noticed how bloody cute he was earlier? Maybe it had something to do with the vast amounts of Labrador flob he'd been covered in, not to mention his mildly shitty attitude.

Amber gave herself a little shake. She needed to remember that no matter how cute Mr William Jones was, he was going to be her manager. Not to mention the fact that she hadn't liked him very much about an hour ago. Amazing how fickle a nicely cut pair of jeans could make you.

'Here,' he said, plonking the mug down in front of her, then sliding into the chair opposite with his own.

'Thanks!' said Amber, picking up the hot drink to stop herself from fiddling with her hair again.

'Look, I wanted to apologise for earlier,' he said, looking at her awkwardly.

'Yeah - me too.'

'What for?!' he said in surprise.

'Setting the hell hounds on you?' she laughed.

'That wasn't your fault. Those two *do* need some serious training though,' he sighed.

Amber shrugged.

'Anyway, sorry I was a bit grumpy. Just took me by surprise.'

'That's fair enough!' said Amber. 'I'm not sure that's anyone's ideal welcome.'

'Well . . . no!'

'So - I spoke to Horace,' said Amber, deciding to get everything out in the open. 'Sounds like we're going to be working together. You're my manager?'

Will's eyes caught hers and held them for a moment. 'You didn't already know?' he asked.

Amber shook her head.

'Right. Well.' He paused and blew on his coffee. 'Look, I think it's best we're open with each other, don't you?'

'O - kay . . .' said Amber, wondering what was coming.

'I don't actually get why you're here,' he said, looking decidedly uncomfortable.

Amber placed her mug back down onto the table a little harder than she'd meant to, but better that than having anything in her hands that she could lob at him too easily.

'You don't *get* why I'm here?' she said, keeping her voice as even as she could.

Will shook his head. 'I mean, how come you can be here for the whole winter? Don't you have other commitments?'

Amber felt her temper start to rise. 'You know that's

totally sexist, right? You're just assuming that because I'm a woman-'

'No, not that!' said Will, looking horrified. 'Sorry, I mean, I heard you had a really busy studio in the village and-'

Amber blew out a frustrated breath. Wasn't this conversation meant to be making things easier - or at least a bit smoother between them? She was pretty sure his backtracking was just him trying to cover his perfectly formed arse, but she'd have to give him the benefit of the doubt, wouldn't she?!

'Yes - I've got a studio down in the craft centre. My friend Emmy has a flower farm in the village so we've decided to share the unit for the winter. She's going to be manning it - selling her own stuff alongside my work and doing some workshops in there while she's at it. So that frees me up to be here.'

Will nodded slowly. 'And you're staying in the house too?'

Amber nodded. 'I've got a room in the west wing.'

'What about your own home?'

'This is it,' she said shortly. What was with this third degree he was giving her?! 'I was lodging with a family and I've given that room up as I won't be there for six months at least. Anyway, they're expecting a new baby.'

'Good timing then,' said Will.

Amber nodded again, still feeling on guard. 'So, does that answer your question as to what I'm doing here?'

Will stared at her. 'Not really.'

Amber made an exasperated sound. 'What do you want to know?!'

'Are you paying rent for your room?'

Amber's mouth dropped open in surprise. 'Not that it's any of your business, but no.'

'And on the paddock?'

'Oh for f-'

'Sorry, but I need to know your motives for being here!'

Amber got to her feet and strode towards the door.

'You can't just walk out on me!' said Will, his voice sharp.

'Stay put,' she growled. 'I'll be back in a minute.'

~

'Here.'

The huge sketchbook and packed lever-arch file made a satisfying thump as she plonked them onto the table directly in front of Will.

'What's this?'

'My motives for being here,' she said, struggling to keep the anger in her voice under control.

Will looked at her in surprise, but Amber just made an annoyed gesture for him to open the sketchbook.

He flipped open the cover, and then slowly leafed through page after page showing the detailed sketches and plans she'd made for the sculpture trail. There was everything in there, from the huge willow sculptures to the living-willow fedges and structures that would hopefully outlive all of them and leave her lasting mark on the landscape of Bamton Hall.

'Beautiful,' said Will simply, as he came to the final page.

'Thanks,' she huffed. 'The costings, equipment, insurance needs and all that boring stuff are in the folder if you want to go through it.'

'I will later. But it still doesn't answer my question. I don't understand why Horace is paying you to be here.'

Feeling's mutual.

'Just for your information, I *am* an RHS gold medal winner.'

'Precisely. He can't afford your fee, so what are you doing here?'

'He's not paying me,' growled Amber. 'Or at least, nothing other than the tiny amount to keep my unit down at the craft centre. The deal is that I have board, lodgings and the use of the paddock for as long as I want it. In return, I put that lot together,' she said pointing at the sketchbook with a finger that was now shaking with the pent up need to throw something at the sanctimonious git.

'For no pay?'

'Look,' she said, struggling to keep a lid on her rising anger, 'this is between me and Horace. It's nothing to do with you.'

'Horace has brought me in to make sure this place is

sorted out. So it's got *everything* to do with me. It doesn't make sense to bring in someone to do a bunch of craft when the estate is-' he paused, looking awkward.

'When the estate is *what?!*' she demanded. She'd pick him up about the craft jibe later. She was too used to that kind of attitude to let it worry her too much, but she was pretty sure he'd been about to let something important slip.

Will just shook his head.

'I thought you said we were going to be open with each other,' she demanded.

He looked at her and then shook his head again.

'Okay - forget that for a sec. What about *your* motives?' she asked. 'Why are you here? Horace implied you're some kind of hotshot.'

Will shrugged. 'I don't have any ties. My old company made me redundant in spite of the hours and years I gave it. There's an ex I'm more than happy to get away from. I'm done with family. With relationships. With ties.'

Amber watched in surprise as he balled his hands up on the table in front of him.

'Anyway - this job came up, and I've known Horace since I was a kid.'

'So he's doing you a favour?' she asked. She knew that it probably wasn't a great idea to prod the bear while he was so wound up - but it was time to see if he could take it as easily as he gave it.

'Yes. Horace is doing me a favour,' he said in a small voice. 'I'm hoping that I'll be able to return that favour several times over while I'm here. Anyway - I aim to just get on with the job - no distractions.'

Amber raised her eyebrows. The guy clearly didn't know just how distracting life in Little Bamton could be.

'Look,' she said, 'I want what's best for Horace and Bamton Hall too. Everything in there,' she said, pointing at the sketchbook, 'is a dream project for me. That's why I'm so happy to do this.'

'And the free paddock? He could be renting that land out.'

Amber spluttered. 'For one thing - *there's no way* he could. Have you even *seen* it? It's basically a bog. The willow will sort that out, dry out the surrounding fields too - making them useable for livestock or whatever - and provide all sorts of other environmental benefits too. All that without the massive cost of restoring the old drainage systems.'

'Great, but-'

'It's all in the folder,' she added quickly. 'And what's with this whole *show me the money!* attitude?' she ploughed on. 'You can't tell me that's coming from Horace!'

Will shook his head, frowning hard. Amber swallowed nervously. Oops, maybe she'd just taken things a little bit too far.

'You're right, it's not coming from Horace,' he

sighed. 'Look - you may as well know exactly what's going on here. This place is in serious financial trouble. If I can't figure out a way to make it pay for itself and turn it around soon, Horace's going to have to sell Bamton Hall.'

Amber froze, staring at Will in horror.

'But then why would he start off these new projects if that's going to happen?' she asked in a small voice. 'Why hire you and get me involved and-'

'Because it doesn't *have* to happen. Not if I can figure out how to turn it all around,' said Will, running his hands roughly through his hair. 'The place isn't in masses of debt - it's just not paying for itself. It's running on a shoestring. Horace has let the local community wander around the grounds for free for years, but that doesn't help with the upkeep! Any issues that come up - Horace is in trouble.'

'Like the tree!' said Amber.

'Exactly,' nodded Will. 'One summer storm, and he's got a tree across the drive that he has to pay to clear. Thank heavens no one was hurt - did you know he didn't have any insurance set up for members of the public to be here?'

Amber shook her head, picked up her coffee but then changed her mind and placed it back on the table. 'Is that the real reason behind closing everything to the public for a while?'

Will nodded. 'Until he can get everything up to scratch for health and safety and get public liability in place, yes. He didn't really have a choice! We just need to keep it all quiet and get a plan in place. Then we can do a "grand reveal" if everything works out.'

'You know, I think you're missing a trick,' said Amber, crossing her arms.

'Of course you do!' sighed Will wearily.

Amber did her best not to growl at him. 'Hear me out. This whole secrecy thing is ridiculous. You don't know this village, but Little Bamton is all about helping each other out - it's what we do. Everyone would want to know that Horace needs help - and they'd rally around!'

'That's really sweet,' said Will, quirking an eyebrow, 'but it's not going to help make the place sustainable, is it?!'

'Look - there are loads of successful, incredible people around here who'd love to be a part of making sure Horace and the hall are safe. They'd be full of ideas - offers of help, support . . .'

'Yeah - all taking their cut at the same time, I'm sure,' muttered Will.

'Bloody hell, what made you so cynical?' Amber demanded.

Will shrugged and shifted uncomfortably in his chair while she watched him intently. She had a feeling that this hard-nosed, cash-grabbing cynic wasn't the real Will Jones . . . but sadly, it was the only version of him she had to work with right now.

'Look,' said Amber, holding up her hands in a

conciliatory gesture and deciding to try another tactic, 'if you're going to do your job here properly and give yourself a chance to succeed - you need to get to know everyone and learn how the village works.'

'I really don't,' he muttered.

'Tough shit, boss,' she said, slapping the table. 'You're coming to the pub with me tonight, no excuses.'

She watched him, wondering whether the flash of anger that crossed his face was going to explode out of him. Maybe she'd just taken things a step too far, but tough. He needed to know from the start that she was someone who spoke her mind, even if he didn't like it.

Saying that, she was mightily relieved when he shot her a sheepish grin instead of bawling her out.

'Fine. I'll come to the pub. You're not allowed to tell anyone any of this though, okay?'

'Not allowed?'

'Horace wouldn't want you to.'

'Okay, okay. I promise. I won't tell anyone. Yet.'

CHAPTER 6

'You must be our mystery man!' beamed Lucy as Amber lead Will straight to the bar.

'Will, this is Lucy - she owns this place and is in my book club too.'

'Nice to meet you,' said Will with a nod and a tight smile.

Crikey, she hoped he'd lighten up a bit! She'd been convinced that he'd back out of this trip all day, but after their rather stormy introductory meeting in the kitchen, she hadn't actually set eyes on Will again until she was heating up a tin of Heinz tomato soup for tea. Not very adventurous, but she'd been walking around the estate most of the afternoon with the dogs, trying to wrap her head around everything he'd told her, and didn't have the energy for anything fancier.

'So - first day at Bamton Hall? How are you settling

in?' asked Lucy as she set to pulling them each a pint of Guinness.

'Not too bad!' said Will. 'At least, it got better after the run-in with the dogs.'

Lucy's eyebrows shot up. 'What did those two monkeys do now?' she asked, looking at Amber.

'Flattened Will and soaked him to the skin,' she said, deciding to leave any mention of badger poop out of the equation.

'Nice. What a lovely welcome!' chuckled Lucy.

'Mmm,' said Will, noncommittally. 'Cheers!' he added, taking the pint from Lucy. 'What do I owe you?'

She shook her head. 'This one's on me - a welcome to Little Bamton drink.'

'That's kind, thanks,' he said, and Amber noticed that his smile was already a lot more relaxed. 'Lucy, can you point me to the gents, please?'

'Course love, just head around the corner there, first on your right.'

The two women watched him go, and as soon as he was around the corner, Lucy turned to Amber and wriggled her eyebrows.

'Well - *he's* not going to be too difficult to work next to!' she grinned. 'What a cutie!'

'Work under,' muttered Amber, 'apparently Horace failed to mention that he's my manager!'

'Under? Even better!'

'Oh hush, you!' said Amber. She didn't blush easily,

but she could feel her face starting to grow hot. 'Anyway, we've already had an almighty bust-up. Twice.'

'What? I thought this was day one for both of you?'

'It is!' said Amber.

'So how have you had two fights already?'

'The dogs,' said Amber, holding up one finger.

'Hardly your fault.'

'I guess I don't blame him so much for that one - they really did flatten him, and then . . .' Amber paused. She'd love nothing more than to pour her heart out to Lucy, but something stopped her.

'Then?' queried Lucy.

Amber shook her head. 'It was nothing. Just a misunderstanding and teething problems.'

Lucy shrugged. 'I wouldn't worry about that if I were you. If he's joined you this evening for a drink, I'd say all is forgiven. Anyway, Horace and Violet will be back before you know it!'

Amber nodded and took a swig of her drink as Lucy moved along the bar to serve Alf, who'd just wandered in.

'Hey, sorry about that!' said Will, sitting back on the stool next to her.

'No worries. So - you've met Lucy. Alf over there is a local farmer, though these days he mostly does horse and cart rides for people with Thor, his gorgeous little Fjord Horse.'

'There are enough people here for that to be profitable?' said Will in surprise.

Amber shrugged. 'The summer gets quite busy - and the craft centre draws loads of people in. Now Emmy's opened Grandad Jim's Flower Farm, and Eve and Finn have started holding art and writing workshops and have the B&B at their place, there's a steady stream of visitors. And of course, Alf and Thor are sometimes booked for weddings too.'

Amber stopped to take another sip of Guinness and instantly wished she'd asked for a packet of crisps too - the tomato soup wasn't proving to have much staying power.

'Weddings, you say?' said Will, looking across at Alf, and then back to her.

Amber looked at him and was surprised to see a little spark in his eyes.

'What?' she said, then cottoning on to where his thoughts were headed she breathed a long, 'oooooh, you mean-'

'Hello lovely!'

Mia's voice behind her made her whip around on her stool and she found herself facing the entire King clan.

'Guys! Fancy seeing you lot here!' laughed Amber.

'Duh,' said Richie, 'you know we come in every Sunday. You always came with us!'

'Duh, I knooooow!' said Amber, reaching her hand out and ruffling his sandy mop.

'Oi! Gerroff!!'

'Hey, I'm Ben,' said Ben, leaning deliberately across the pair of them and holding out his hand.

'Will,' said Will with a grin.

'This is my wife, Mia, and our kids Richie and Belle.'

'Hi guys,' said Will.

'I'm not a guy!' piped up Belle, who was now leaning her elbows on Amber's lap. 'Do you live in the princess castle with Amber?'

Will shot a quick glance at Amber, who gave him a little nod. 'She means Bamton Hall,' she whispered.

'Yep, sure do!' said Will. 'How do you know Amber?'

'She lived with us ever since I was just two years old, but then she had to move out and live in a princess castle with you. We made her cookies.'

'They were excellent cookies,' said Will very seriously, 'Amber shared one with me.'

'Then you must be special,' breathed Belle.

Mia let out a snort and Richie rolled his eyes.

'What do you mean, Belle?' chuckled Ben.

"Cause Amber only shares her food with special people.'

'From the mouths of babes!' laughed Amber, dropping a kiss onto Belle's head. When she looked up, she couldn't help but notice the soft smile that Will was giving Belle.

'So, have you been to Bamton Hall before?' he asked, and Amber was taken by the way he was talking to the little girl instead of directly over her head.

'She has, but she was too little to remember,' said

Richie. 'I've been though. I love it. We went paddling in the stream.'

'Yeah,' laughed Amber, 'so did Diesel and Tarmac earlier. Actually, more like a bath to get rid of the badger poo.'

'Gross!' said Richie, his eyes lighting up.

'Yup - they stank,' laughed Will.

'Wiiiiiilll,' said Belle, staring at him.

'Yes?' he said, looking delighted as Belle took his hand.

'Amber said I could come up to the castle for a princess sleepover. Can I still come?'

Will glanced at Amber, and for a second she couldn't read the look on his face. 'If Amber says yes, then I'm sure you can.'

'Wiiiiiillll?'

'Yes?'

'Are you Amber's boyfriend?'

Amber nearly sprayed her sip of Guinness right across the bar.

'Belle!' said Mia, looking horrified. 'Will, I'm so sorry, I don't know where she picks these things up from!'

'That's okay!' Will replied, gaining definite brownie points for the fact that he was laughing instead of trying to crawl under the bar in embarrassment. 'No, I'm Amber's friend.'

Belle nodded seriously. 'Then you can make me hot chocolate when I come to stay.'

The way she said it was so final it brooked no refusal. Amber simply shook her head in amusement.

'Okay. Deal,' said Will. 'You coming up to stay too?' he asked, turning to Richie.

'Only if I don't have to dress up like a princess,' he muttered.

Will grinned at him. 'Sounds like a plan to me.'

'Richie's going to be helping me out a bit when I get started!' said Amber.

Will widened his eyes at her - clearly worried that she was going to start spreading state secrets.

'Don't worry,' said Richie, 'she won't tell me what we're going to be doing - but I know it'll be something to do with willow, otherwise Amber wouldn't be interested.'

'Cheers, mate!' laughed Amber.

'He does have a point,' said Ben.

'Right, you horrors, let's leave these two alone to enjoy their drink.'

∽

By the time she'd introduced Will to what felt like the entire village, apart from Sue who hadn't appeared yet, Amber was pretty much tired of having to tell people that - no - Will wasn't her new boyfriend. It seemed that Belle wasn't the only one who had *no* problem in asking the awkward question. Amber had laughed it off each time, but she had the definite sense that Will's good humour would only stretch so far and might already be wearing a little thin for one evening.

She couldn't say she blamed him - it had been a long and rather bizarre day. Amber had to admit that she was more than ready to head back to the relative peace and quiet of Bamton Hall, let the boys out for a quick run around, and then settle in for an early night.

'Luce?' she said as her friend bustled past with a tray, 'is Sue not in tonight? I really wanted to introduce Will before we headed off.'

Lucy nodded. 'Yeah - she should be here in about five minutes.'

'Cool.'

Amber peered around for Will, only to find him deep in conversation with Mark, Little Bamton's lovely vicar. It always made her smile to see Mark in here on a Sunday evening, but she'd heard him claim many times that some of his most important community work was done in the pub on a Sunday evening.

'Evening, vicar,' she smiled as she reached their table.

'Hi Amber, how're the new digs?'

'Beautiful, thanks,' she said. 'I see you two've already met?'

Will nodded. 'Mark was just telling me the same storm that brought down the tree at Bamton Hall also meant the Summer Fete had to be cancelled.'

'Yeah - that was such a shame,' said Amber. 'Sue was

gutted. She does most of the organisation for it - it's a lot of work to go to waste like that!'

'Did I hear my name mentioned in vain?'

Sue appeared at Amber's shoulder and threw an arm around her.

'Hi!' grinned Amber. 'This is Will - he's Bamton Hall's new Estate Manager!'

'Ooh, the mystery man!' said Sue. 'Nice to meet you.'

'You too - and that's the second time I've been called that tonight.'

Mark laughed. 'You'll have to excuse us, Will. A newcomer in a small village like ours is always big news - and Horace didn't share many details about you - so there's been a lot of chatter. I'm guessing your ears have been burning!'

'So, tell us - what were you up to before moving to the hall?' said Sue.

Amber glanced at her friend. She didn't quite sound her usual, cheerful self for some reason. Maybe it was her imagination, but it almost sounded like she was challenging Will.

Will just shrugged. 'I managed properties for a couple of large companies. Made sure the right people were doing the right things.'

'You sound like a handy guy to have around!' laughed Mark.

'I tended to be more on the management end of

things - figuring out what needed to be done and who had the skills to do it.'

'So, not getting your hands *too* dirty then?' said Sue.

This time Amber *knew* she wasn't imagining things - something that was confirmed by the look of mild surprise that crossed the vicar's face as he reached for his drink. What on earth had gotten into her usually down-to-earth, kind friend?

'No. I guess you could say that,' said Will. He smiled at her, but Amber noticed that it didn't meet his eyes this time.

Perhaps it wasn't just her that felt enough was enough for one night. 'I'm just going to nip to the loo, and then maybe we could call it a night, Will? I'm wiped!'

Will nodded, sending her a grateful glance. 'Sounds like a plan.'

CHAPTER 7

*A*mber strode back towards the hall with a chocolate Labrador trotting along on either side of her. It was like some kind of miracle had happened over the last few days - the boys were actually starting to behave themselves. She wasn't sure if it was extra walks and constant fresh air that was doing the trick - they'd been outside with her all day every day as she started to mark out the sites for her sculptures - or whether it was more the fact that she simply wouldn't tolerate their bad behaviour in the same way Horace did. Either way, it was a blessed relief, and Tarmac and Diesel were actually turning out to be excellent company now that they weren't in constant destructo-mode.

In fact, Amber was incredibly glad of their company given that she'd barely seen Will since their drink down at the pub on Sunday. They'd briefly passed each other in the kitchen, but he was never still for more than five minutes at a time. *Not* that she was looking for his company of course, but - well - she'd rather liked the version of him she'd seen in the pub, and she wouldn't have minded getting to know him a bit better. Or a lot better.

'Stop it, Amber!' she muttered, cross with herself. 'Come on lads, I reckon you two can join me for breakfast in the kitchen this morning.'

She wandered around to the side door and the boys followed her into the hallway. She didn't bother clipping their leads on as they'd taken to following her calmly, rather than trying to wreck the joint at every given opportunity.

Amber had to admit that she rather hoped Will might be down in the kitchen this morning. Not that she was trying to accidentally-on-purpose bump into him or anything, but with Horace and Violet due to return tomorrow, it *would* be quite handy to get her sketchbook and folder back from him. Not to mention that she was dying to get an update from Will about his plans. She'd really hoped that meeting everyone down in the village might have inspired him a bit, but Sue's less than friendly demeanour had put a bit of a dampener on that plan.

Amber still wasn't one hundred per cent certain what that had been about. All she knew was that when she'd come back from the loo, Will had retreated fully into his shell, Sue was nowhere to be seen, and it was a rather embarrassed-looking Lucy who'd wished them both good night.

Amber couldn't get her head around it. She'd known Sue for years, and she'd always been lovely - easy-going, patient and very loyal - one of the stalwarts of Little Bamton. She was always ready to lend a hand wherever she could. After all, she'd won Lucy's heart, and that was no mean feat in itself.

Then, of course, on the other side of this particular equation was Will. Even though Amber had only just met him, she'd already witnessed first-hand just how prickly he could be. Saying that - it had definitely been Sue who'd started in on him and not the other way around.

No matter - as soon as Eve was back from London, Amber had promised to invite the girls up to the hall for a special-edition book club meeting. She'd grill Sue and get to the bottom of all this - if she hadn't managed to winkle it out of Will before then. *If* she ever managed to pin the man down.

Mmm. She really did have to stop imagining pinning Will down.

Amber paused at a mirror in the hallway and quickly made sure she didn't have mud on her face and her hair wasn't in some kind of weird, windswept Mohican. Not that it mattered, but . . .

Oh, who was she kidding? *It mattered!* If she did happen to bump into Will, she wanted to look at least halfway decent. It was probably because she'd had way too much time to herself this week with just the dogs to talk to, but she couldn't get that blasted man out of her head.

Knowing he was around the estate somewhere meant that she'd been checking over her shoulder almost as often as she'd checked her reflection - and it just wasn't like her! But there was something about him. The way he'd been with the kids when he'd met them down at the pub kept making her go all wibbly, and she wasn't used to it. She wasn't even sure she liked the feeling.

Amber forced herself to stop fiddling with her hair and looked down at the two dogs who were sitting at her feet looking like butter wouldn't melt. 'No, *you* like him!' she muttered at them, before patting her thighs and heading for the kitchen.

The sooner she could make a proper start on these blasted sculptures, the better. She needed some good, physical work to take her mind off William Jones.

Pushing open the door to the kitchen, she was surprised to find that the man himself was already there, busy with his back to her over at the counter.

'Oh, hi Will,' she said, shrugging off her coat as the dogs trotted over to hoover up any spilt crumbs from around his feet.

Will swung around, keeping his hands raised so that the dogs couldn't lick them.

'What are you up to?!' she said in surprise, eyeballing the blue and white striped apron he was wearing and the fact that his hands were coated in flour.

'Making bread!' he said with a sheepish grin. 'Thought it might be a nice welcome home for Horace - and we've nearly run out.'

'Wow,' said Amber. 'There's dedication for you!'

'Hardly,' laughed Will, turning back and continuing to knead the large lump of dough in front of him. 'I do it to relax. I always used to make bread with mum when I was a kid. It's a habit that stuck.'

'Relax? Really?' she said. 'Cooking stresses me out.'

'Hence the Heinz soup addiction?' he laughed.

Amber grinned. 'Yup.'

'Well, there'll be fresh bread to go with it tonight.'

'Can't say no to that!'

'Well . . .' said Will, neatly balling the dough, popping it back into a huge mixing bowl, draping a checked tea towel over the top and setting it aside to prove, 'maybe you'll say no in favour of some home-made pizza?'

Amber's mouth instantly started to water. 'Really?'

'Do you like mushrooms?'

'Yup!'

'Then a simple mushroom and mozzarella pizza? I think there's a jar of olives in the fridge if you want to go crazy?'

'Deal! Thanks Will!'

'No probs - it's my way of saying thank you,' he said, shooing the dogs out of his way so that he could cross over to the huge Belfast sink and wash the flour off his hands.

'Say thank you for what?' she asked.

'I'd really like to sound you out on some ideas before Horace gets back.'

'Ideas for Bamton Hall?'

Will nodded. 'I was thinking about what you said.'

'Steady on,' she laughed, 'don't go making a habit of it!'

He shrugged. 'You were right - this place needs its local community - not just to survive, but to thrive. But breakfast first?'

Amber nodded. 'Cornflakes, here I come,' she said a little less than enthusiastically as her stomach grumbled.

'Fancy a freshly baked chocolate chip muffin and coffee instead?'

'Why, is opening a Costa at Bamton Hall one of your plans?' she laughed, then she quickly glared at him as a drop of fear landed in her stomach. 'It's not, is it?'

Will chuckled. 'No, but I'll add it to my list!'

'Don't you dare,' she breathed. 'Forget I said it!'

'Okay. But muffin and coffee?'

'Really?'

Will shrugged, grabbed the oven mitts and carefully lifted six perfect muffins out of the oven.

'Okay - you're a keeper,' said Amber, then promptly felt like someone had emptied a bucket of hot water over her head. 'Shit, I just said that out loud, didn't I?'

Will nodded, looking like he was doing his best to stop a laugh from escaping. 'Let me guess,' he said, 'forget you said it?'

'Yup,' said Amber, her voice curt as she wished that she had long hair so that she could hide her burning cheeks behind it. 'Come on boys,' she said, grabbing the large dishes from their feeding mat, 'let's get you both sorted out first.'

~

Two muffins and two cups of strong coffee later, Amber was simply hoping that the double-threat coffee and sugar high wouldn't make her act the idiot . . . because she had the feeling that they'd now moved onto the serious part of proceedings.

'Okay, you ready?' said Will, leaning back in his chair after draining the dregs of his coffee, and resting one hand on Tarmac's head as he plonked it in Will's lap.

'Ready, boss,' she said with a smirk.

'Really, we're doing the whole "boss" thing?' he said screwing up his nose.

Amber shrugged. 'Up to you.'

'Then nope, definitely not.'

Definite brownie points. The man was on fire this morning.

'So - I think you were right - it's not about looking

for areas where Bamton Hall can cut back on existing spending because, well-'

'Horace hasn't spent anything on the place and that's actually part of the problem?'

'Right,' nodded Will. 'And before we go any further, this is the part where I apologise for being so rude when I was asking about what you were charging and whether you were paying rent to stay here.'

'Thanks - but it's fine,' said Amber.

'No, it's not. I was really worried about Horace - still am, if I'm honest - and it made me way more blunt than I should have been, and I'm sorry.'

Amber smiled at him. 'Apology accepted.'

'Alright.'

'I'm sorry too, by the way,' said Amber. 'I *do* get why you're here. I just hope we can make it work!'

Will smiled at her. 'On with the plans, then. So - three things I thought we could do to start with. The first is obvious - we get on with the work we've both been brought in here to do anyway. I've looked through your notes, all the costings and your sketchbook. It's going to be a huge draw if we give it some publicity, and it's pretty sustainable. There's some maintenance, obviously, but-'

'But that's part of the deal with me getting to use the paddock,' she said.

'Right. So the only real cost is the materials - willow and the steel armatures for inside the sculptures.'

'Yep - but my mate's welding those up for me for

practically nothing because I promised to do a weaving workshop for his kid's birthday party next year!'

'Does this entire village work on a barter system?' asked Will, looking impressed.

Amber shrugged. 'Pretty much!'

'Well, that's win-win. Though it does seem like you're giving up a lot of your personal time for this project.'

Amber shrugged again. 'It's my time to give.'

Will stared at her for a moment before carrying on. 'As for my side of things, I've had a proper look around the property. The cost of sorting out the boundaries so that Horace can let some of the fields to local farmers is higher than I'd have thought. They're in a state.'

'Oh dear,' said Amber.

'Yep. So that possible bit of income would be more than gobbled up. In terms of re-opening the gardens and grounds nearer the house, I think we'd need some proper signage and designated paths to stop people going literally everywhere. Mainly because then at least we can focus the maintenance and health and safety in those areas?'

Amber nodded. It made sense but sounded like it'd cost a packet too.

'There are several trees that we'd need to have looked at to make sure they're safe, and possibly have some work done on them if they're not. I haven't priced that up yet but-'

'It sounds expensive,' sighed Amber. Already, the

lovely sugar high she'd been enjoying after scoffing her muffins was turning into something that felt far more like anxiety. 'Okay - so part one of your plan has got me thoroughly depressed.'

'I know,' he sighed. 'That's where I got to as well. Any comments before I move on?'

'Yes - please tell me the next two parts are more cheerful?'

Will smiled at her. 'Depends on how you look at them. But before that - any other comments?'

'Well,' said Amber. 'This might be obvious, and it's only a suggestion-'

'All suggestions very welcome - trust me!'

'Okay, so you mentioned how things here work a bit on a bit of a barter system - well, perhaps a local farmer might be willing to pay to re-fence certain areas of the estate in return for using those fields free of charge for a set number of years. That way the farmer is still paying to rent them but the payment goes straight to the fencing company . . .'

Will nodded slowly. 'So the work gets done, the farmer gets to use the fields, but Bamton Hall's left in a better shape even after the time's up on the agreement. You know - that might just work if Horace goes for it.'

'And as for the paths and signs and trees, I bet you someone in the village knows someone who could help, or might have an idea that would help or . . .'

'Well, we can definitely work on that. But it does lead me to idea number two.'

'Hit me!'

'We hold an Autumn Fayre here to make up for the fact that the village Summer Fete got cancelled.'

Amber gaped at him. 'I don't get it. I mean, that's a lovely idea and everything, but tons of extra work and . . .'

'It would get the entire village back up here way sooner than we're ready to open back up fully - but in a controlled, one-off event. Plus I was thinking that maybe there could be an element included that would raise a bit of money for the work we need to do at the hall.'

'Any profit from the Summer Fete usually gets split between the Church Fund and a nominated charity.'

Will nodded. 'Yes, Mark told me. He also told me that the Church Fund will run short this year because of the loss of that donation, and as I understand it, it's used to benefit the village?'

Amber nodded.

'So if we do a fayre up here, it would be mostly in aid of the Church Fund, but we'd include a couple of things to raise money for Bamton Hall - and we'd be really open about how much we need to raise, and make sure it's used for the bits of maintenance that are all about welcoming our local community back.'

Amber was nodding slowly, 'like the new paths and safety work on the trees?'

Will nodded, grinning. 'And we'll be helping Mark

out too - and the village. Do you reckon we might get some help and support from the locals?'

Amber nodded. 'Definitely.'

'And . . . do you think you could ask Sue if she might be willing to share her wisdom? I erm . . . I *would* ask her myself, but I got the sense she didn't like me much!' he said.

Amber stared at him and for a moment it was impossible to miss the flash of hurt that crossed his face.

'You know - I'm not sure that was about you . . . it's so unlike her, so out of character . . .'

'But you'll ask her?' he prompted

'Of course,' said Amber, getting the distinct feeling he'd like to change the subject. 'We'll need all the help we can get to pull it off!'

'Thanks.'

'Okay, number three?' asked Amber.

'For that, we need to go for a walk.'

∽

'And here we are - the most screwed up room in the entire hall!' laughed Amber, stretching her arms wide and spinning on the spot as she took in the state of the library.

Sure, it was a lot better than it had been that first morning, with soot, ash and most of the guts of the old sofa liberally spread across the room, but it was still pretty shabby. There were cobwebs in every nook and cranny, the old carpet was threadbare, the windows needed a good wash, and the overwhelming odour of damp Labrador seemed to cling to the room.

She watched as the not-so-terrible two did a couple of laps of their space, had a quick bounce on the half-eaten sofa and then flopped down on their bed to sleep off their breakfasts.

'Please tell me you're not planning on opening this as a community library or something,' she said, raising an eyebrow at Will.

He shook his head. 'I need you to look past the top several layers and look at the beautiful light pouring in through those windows. The view across the gardens. That beautiful stained glass at the top of the arch there.'

'O-kay,' said Amber, raising her eyebrows.

'And that fireplace - in the summer, it could be filled with flowers and in the winter, full of pillar candles!'

'Riiight? I'm still not getting it!' she said, looking at him in confusion.

In response he grabbed one of her hands and, looking excited, tugged her over so that they stood, awkwardly facing each other in front of the dogs' bed.

'Imagine soft music, maybe a string quartet. A willow arch overhead covered with flowers, and instead of two troublesome hounds,' he glanced down at the dogs, who were both sitting up now, clearly interested in this new game that was unfolding, 'instead of them, there'd be a registrar.'

'Weddings?' said Amber. 'In here?'

Will nodded, looking pleased with himself.

Amber looked around her, doing her best to peer past the layers of dust, dog and dirt to imagine what this room could be like.

He was right. It could be really beautiful. Old-world, slightly bookish, a bit of a fairy tale filled with flowers.

'Is that even a possibility?' she asked, looking back at him, her voice slightly husky as she did her best not to focus too hard on the fact that he was still holding her hand.

Will nodded. 'I've spoken to the council. Totally doable. The venue licence - the "grant of approval" - isn't massively expensive. And, from what I've seen, we've already got a lot of what a bride would want in the village - flowers, a horse and cart, B&B for guests and . . .'

Amber was doing her best not to get distracted by the fact that as he got more and more excited, his hand kept squeezing hers. It was doing something funny to her insides.

'And?' she prompted, her voice sounding hoarse.

'And I was thinking that, if Horace likes the idea and really wanted to build a business here, he could actually use the whole of the West Wing as a wedding venue. Turn one of those beautiful, big bedrooms into a bridal suite. Have our living room turned into somewhere for the wedding breakfast. What do you think?'

Amber looked around her again. She could see it as clear as day. She could imagine the newlyweds posing under her willow arch for photographs before heading out into the grounds for more photos amongst the flowers and her sculptures.

'I love it! I- oops!' she let out a little squeal as Tarmac, clearly bored of being imprisoned in his bed, bulldozed his way straight into the back of her legs and toppled her right into Will. He caught her on reflex, both his arms wrapping around her as they stared into each other's eyes, mere inches apart.

'Sorry,' she muttered.

'No worries.'

Neither of them moved.

'I should-'

'Right!'

Still neither of them moved, and for just a second, Amber thought Will was going to kiss her. Clearly, all this talk of weddings had gone straight to both their heads.

At last, Will loosened his grip. 'Okay?' he said.

'Yeah, thanks,' she smiled at him, though something that felt worryingly like disappointment coursed through her as he finally let go.

CHAPTER 8

'See,' said Violet, turning and poking one bony finger into Horace's chest. 'I *told* you if we left these two together for a couple of days, they'd have Bamton Hall straightened out by the time we got back!'

Horace smiled down at Violet, and a little lump formed in Amber's throat as she watched him wind one arm around her shoulders. The pair of them had only become an item a couple of months ago, after taking Eve's art workshop together, but they came across like an old married couple. Violet loved bossing Horace around, and he seemed to love being bossed.

The four of them were standing together in the library. Well, actually, it was more like the *six* of them, as Tarmac and Diesel had been glued to Horace's side ever since he came home, and even now sat at his feet, staring up at him in adoration, completely ignoring Violet.

'Yes. I have to say I do love your plans,' said Horace. 'I know a couple of local chaps who've been after use of some of the further fields for a couple of years now. Lovely fellows too - I know they'd look after the land, and it's just the sort of thing they might jump at as they do all their boundary work themselves - so wouldn't be so much of an outlay for them.'

'Maybe we can have a chat with them together?' said Will.

'Over a pint! Good plan.'

Violet rolled her eyes at Amber, and she couldn't help but laugh.

'I like the idea of having an Autumn Fayre up here,' said Violet. 'Lovely to support the Church Fund. Do you think everyone would feel it's a bit cheeky to be raising cash for the hall too?'

Will shrugged. 'I wondered that - but if it was something like, I don't know - like a weaving stall where Amber was showing people how to make something simple? And we were really honest about what the money was going to be spent on - like work on the trees or public pathways, I don't think anyone would have a problem with it.'

Amber nodded. 'I think you should have donation buckets on the gate too - and split those fifty-fifty.'

'So - the fayre is a definite yes,' said Horace. 'So's the possibility of letting some fields to get the fences fixed. Obviously your sculptures are a done deal, Amber. The one thing I need to think over for a while longer is this wedding idea.' He ran his hand through his hair and stared around at the library. 'I'd miss this room.'

'It wouldn't be gone,' laughed Violet. 'It just wouldn't be a doggy hell-hole!'

Amber laughed.

'Yes, I know, but . . . it wouldn't be the same, would it? It's not a no - I just need to think about the logistics of the whole of the West Wing being full of strangers.'

'Not all the time,' said Will. 'Things like weddings are booked way in advance, so you'd know when there were guests due, and you could block any days in the bookings calendar that you definitely wouldn't want people here.'

Horace nodded. 'Let me have a think about it. I can see exactly what you're saying - and I agree it would make a beautiful place to get married. It's quite a change though, so I just need a bit of time to wrap my head around it.'

'Of course. There's plenty that we have to get on with before then anyway!' laughed Will. 'Especially if we're going to make a go of the fayre. When do you think we should hold it?'

'Halloween,' said Violet decidedly. 'I don't usually hold with all that nonsense, but it would give it a wonderful theme and the chance for costume competitions and all that, apple bobbing, pumpkin carving . . . or turnips if you can't get the pumpkins!'

'Great idea, though that doesn't give us very much time!' said Will looking concerned.

'Don't worry,' said Violet, 'I like a challenge. I'll get an army of helpers together. If you can make sure that it's all insured and safe, I'll do my best to make sure that we spend as little as humanly possible.'

'Deal,' said Will, looking thrilled.

'You know, I really am impressed with everything you two've done over the past few days,' said Horace.

Amber glanced at him and suddenly had the sneaking suspicion that he hadn't really been listening - he was too busy fussing Diesel and Tarmac.

'The only thing is,' he continued, 'I think you might have broken my dogs!'

'What?' she gasped. 'Why, what's wrong with them?' She cast a horrified look at the two dogs, who were still staring lovingly up at Horace. Sure, she'd more than exceeded their daily treat allowance - though she'd swapped to a more natural alternative - but they'd deserved it!

'Well,' said Horace, 'they're sitting still, for a start! And when I got back earlier, I didn't get knocked off my feet once. Plus - there's still a little bit of stuffing left in that sofa. They're off their game!'

'I promise I'm not drugging them,' laughed Amber. 'They've just been getting tons of exercise and fresh air as I've kept them outside with me all day. I didn't want them destroying the hall while I wasn't looking!'

'Yes, plenty of exercise instead of eating treats and watching old black and white films with you,' laughed Violet. 'Plus, I doubt Amber puts up with their nonsense in quite the same way - you spoil them rotten!'

'We enjoy our films, don't we lads?' said Horace fondly, laying a hand on each silky head. 'Though, I must say it *is* rather lovely to have you in a room for ten minutes without you destroying something.'

～

With the fayre having been given the go-ahead for Halloween, Amber decided that it was high time to get her stuff together and start weaving. She'd had a chat with Will, and they'd both agreed that she'd work on completing the two sculptures that were due to be situated on the side lawn first. This was where the fayre would mostly be taking place, and they would make a striking centrepiece to proceedings, and hopefully build a bit of excitement for the project amongst the locals.

First things first. Amber had a huge willow delivery arriving the next afternoon from her supplier, who'd readily agreed to deliver it up to Bamton Hall as she was such a regular customer. Her plan was to get the willow she needed for the first sculpture on to soak straight away - she didn't have any time to lose. Then she really needed to collect the two steel armatures from her friend Danny.

She'd given him a call to find out how the work was going, and although he told her that he hadn't finished all the welding work, now that she knew which two she needed to start with, he agreed to get them ready for her to pick up in a few days.

After thanking him profusely, Amber hung up and tried to figure out how on earth she was going to get the things from the neighbouring town up to the hall. It didn't really matter that her car was still in the garage - there was no way the inner workings of what would become a seven-foot warrior maiden with a bow and arrow, along with a full-sized wild boar, would fit in the back of her Ford. Nor Horace's Land Rover for that matter.

It didn't take too long for the brainwave to hit her. Time to kill multiple birds with one stone.

'Sue? It's Amber!'

'Hello lovely - this *is* a surprise. How's it going up there?'

'Totally mad,' said Amber truthfully, looking around at the cavernous kitchen and twirling the spiral phone cord nervously around her finger. She'd resorted to using Horace's landline after her mobile had cut out three times while she'd been talking to Danny.

'Anything I can do to help?' asked Sue straight away.

Amber wanted to hug her friend. 'Funny you should ask that, I was calling to ask for a huge favour.'

'Go on . . .'

'I've got to pick up two bits of steel-work the day after tomorrow. Because it's such short notice, Danny can't bring them to me. I was wondering-'

'We'll just take my truck!' said Sue, cutting across her.

'You're an angel!' said Amber gratefully.

'It's no problem at all - I'm not working that day anyway, so I'm all yours. What time?'

'If we could head over in the morning, that would be amazing. Then I can get them in place and ready to start work.'

'Sure! We'll pick them up, I'll treat us to a breakfast bap - and then we can get them unloaded at your end right where you need them.'

'Sounds perfect - but the baps are on me!'

~

'So, how's it going with the new boy?' demanded Sue as soon as they pulled out of Bamton Hall.

Amber was surprised. She'd half expected Sue to avoid the subject entirely after what had happened when the pair of them had first met. In fact -

'Sue, what happened that night at the pub?'

'I don't know what you mean,' said Sue, not taking her eyes off the narrow road.

'Oh, come on,' laughed Amber. 'I've never seen you like that before.'

Sue glanced at her. 'Okay. There was just something about him I wasn't sure about, and he put me on my guard.'

'Your guard?' laughed Amber. 'You were busy giving

him the third degree, and then when I came back from the loo, you'd done a runner and I could barely get a word out of the guy.'

Sue shrugged. 'Sorry, I just didn't trust him.'

'Why ever not?' said Amber.

'Didn't you notice he didn't actually answer any of my questions fully - I mean, everything was vague. He "made sure the right people were doing the right jobs". He "managed properties".'

'So? Some jobs are like that.'

'Has he told you *anything* about himself? I mean, *really* told you?'

Amber thought for a moment. 'He used to bake bread with his mum and still does it when he needs to relax,' she said, a triumphant note in her voice.

'That's very sweet,' said Sue, 'but I meant more about the professional side of things.'

Amber shook her head. 'No. We've talked about Bamton Hall and our plans for that. And how we're going to save . . .' Amber paused. Shit, she wasn't sure if she was supposed to mention anything about the hall struggling.

'Save it? Is that what you were going to say?' demanded Sue.

Amber suddenly wished that the pair of them were anywhere other than stuck together in the cab of Sue's truck. There was no escape, and there was no way she was willing to lie to her friend either.

'Yes,' said Amber in a small voice.

'Horace is in trouble? Is there a chance he's going to lose the hall?'

Amber sighed. 'He's not in trouble - but I think there's a good chance he'd be forced to sell up unless he can make Bamton Hall work for him very soon.'

'But he gets loads of visitors. Everyone loves Bamton Hall,' said Sue.

Amber nodded and then decided she may as well be completely honest now that she'd let the cat out of the bag. 'Yes - loads of visitors, all there for free. And he hasn't got health and safety sorted, nor proper insurance, and no real way that the estate is doing anything other than costing him money.'

'Jeez. Poor Horace! So then - is that why he's got Will on board?'

Amber nodded. 'Yep - he's there to figure out what needs doing, how much it's going to cost and how to pay for it.'

'And you? I mean this in the nicest possible way but-'

'I know,' said Amber. 'Horace had this idea for me to create a sculpture trail around the gardens so that there was a new attraction to draw people back in when it's re-opened.'

'But surely that's going to cost him, and not necessarily bring any money in?' said Sue.

Amber did her best not to feel too nettled. 'Yeah. I mean, I'm not charging him my time - but he's covering the unit for me, and I've got somewhere to stay and food and all that . . .'

'I didn't mean it like that,' sighed Sue. 'You deserve every penny of any fee you charge for your beautiful work. I just meant-'

'I know,' said Amber, briefly touching Sue's arm. 'Sorry, I've just been feeling a bit touchy about the whole thing.'

'Has Will made you feel like that?' Sue demanded.

Amber looked at her in surprise. 'No - not at all! We did have a very blunt conversation about it all on our first day up there, but since then, he's been brilliant.'

'Oh. Okay.'

'No - I mean, I feel a bit bad because my side of things is something that Horace agreed to before he really faced up to the fact that he needed to make some changes.'

'And what are these changes?' demanded Sue.

They were already coming up to the outskirts of the industrial estate where Danny's workshop stood, and Amber couldn't wait to make a break from the truck but before then, she needed to be straight with Sue. After all, a large part of their plan was dependent on her help.

'Well. Horace has to start making an income from the hall. It's got to at least help pay for itself, otherwise he'll be forced to sell.'

'And he wants to stay there?'

Amber was surprised by the question. 'I assume so. I mean, I've not actually asked him . . .'

'Has anyone?'

Amber shrugged. 'I can't see why he'd get Will involved - or me, for that matter - if what he actually wanted to do was sell.'

'Okay. Fair point.'

'I really do think he just wants to show the place off at its best and share it with the community he loves so much.'

'So he gets some business whizz-kid in to do that? It just doesn't seem right. There's something going on there.'

Amber shook her head. 'There really isn't. Will's dad's a close friend of Horace's. He was made redundant from his last job, and . . .' she was going to add about his throwaway mention of needing a break from his ex, but quickly decided against it. For whatever reason, Sue didn't like Will, so it didn't seem fair to share personal details with her. 'And so he was available to help,' she finished.

'And what grand plans has he had?'

'Get insurance and health and safety sorted, and proper pathways and signage to open back up to the public - and show off my new sculptures,' said Amber.

'Well, that's just common sense. What else?'

'Horace hasn't okayed this yet - but there are talks about turning the West Wing into a wedding venue.'

She saw Sue raise her eyebrows at this. 'Where would you hold the ceremonies?'

'The library,' said Amber.

'I haven't seen it for years, but last time I did it was a kind of man-cave with added dog!' said Sue with a smirk.

'Still is,' laughed Amber, 'but under all that, it's a lovely room. Will pointed out that amazing window that looks out over the garden would be a gorgeous backdrop, and then there's the open fireplace, and wooden floor and . . .'

'He's right,' said Sue grudgingly. 'But surely that would take some serious work to make it happen?'

'Some, but he's already spoken to the council.'

'Fair play. But that's long-game stuff. What about short-term?'

'Well, he wants to hold an Autumn Fayre up at Bamton Hall,' said Amber in a rush, as they pulled into Danny's yard at the back of his workshop. 'To make up for the fact that the Summer Fete was cancelled.'

Sue yanked on the handbrake and turned to stare at her.

'He what?!'

'He was talking to Mark in the pub - and he'd really like to help out the Church Fund by making it happen. We'd add in a couple of things to make some funds for the work that's needed up at the hall too.'

'So you'd invite the whole village back up to Bamton Hall?' said Sue.

'Well, yes. To start with, we were going to try to be hush-hush about everything up there and then have this big reveal of the new, improved hall when it was ready to re-open. But I think Will's come to see that if everyone realises Horace and Bamton hall need their support, Little Bamton will rally around.'

'Of course we will. Hush-hush indeed. How ridiculous! That's the problem with bringing in an outsider,' snorted Sue. 'Well, it'll be a lot of hard work.'

Amber nodded.

'When's he planning on holding it?'

'Halloween,' she muttered.

'In that case,' said Sue, 'you're going to need my help.'

CHAPTER 9

'Wait, you're telling me she *volunteered* to help?' said Will, grabbing one end of the heavy metal trough and helping Amber to shift it a few feet closer to the gardener's hut.

'Yup!' said Amber, stretching her back as they set it down. 'Though - I have to warn you - I think it was more so that she could spend some time up here and keep an eye on . . . things.'

'And by things, you mean me?' said Will.

Amber nodded. 'Sorry. I still don't know what's gotten into her. She's got some kind of bee in her bonnet, but even *she* had to admit that your wedding venue plan was a good idea.'

'You told her?' said Will.

Amber shot him a look. He didn't look angry, just surprised.

'Look, we needed her help, and Sue has a sharp nose

for any kind of bullshit so it just made sense to be open with her. And anyway - she won't say a word to anyone until Horace agrees to the plan. I made her promise.'

Will shrugged and Amber breathed a sigh of relief. She really didn't understand Sue's problem with Will - apart from the fact that he still had a way to go in cottoning on to how things worked around here. He just hadn't quite grasped that loyalty and looking after their own was a huge part of village life - even when it came to something as huge as helping Horace keep hold of Bamton Hall.

'Come on - one more to go!' said Will, nodding over at the last trough.

They ambled towards it, neither of them in a hurry to lift it. They'd yanked them off the back of the old Land Rover as close to where Amber wanted them as possible - but it still meant shifting the blasted things into position. At least she'd be able to get the willow for the first sculpture on to soak, though. The rule was you had to soak it for one day per foot of length. She'd be able to make a proper start soon now that the armatures were anchored in place.

'Will . . .'

'Mmm?'

'Has Horace actually said that he *wants* to stay here at Bamton Hall?'

'What?' Will drew to an abrupt halt and turned to stare at her.

'I mean, we're doing all this in the hopes of the hall

becoming more sustainable - so that he can keep hold of it, right?'

Will nodded.

'Well, has anyone asked him if that's what *he* wants.'

'I . . . erm . . . no - if I'm honest, I haven't,' said Will.

Amber glanced at him, and suddenly Sue's warnings were ringing in her ears again. He looked uncomfortable. Maybe Sue was right about one thing - Will *was* hiding something.

'Oh,' she said, deciding not to push the point right now. 'Fair enough.'

'I mean, it wouldn't have got to this point if Horace didn't want to stay here, would it? He'd have just got estate agents involved.'

'I guess so,' said Amber.

'Seriously - what would have stopped him? He'd already closed the gardens to the public. He could have just said he wanted to downsize, put the place up for sale and that would have been that. I mean - even if he couldn't get a private sale, there are plenty of companies that would snap up a place like this.'

Amber nodded. He was right, of course. Maybe Sue's strange mistrust had rubbed off on her and she was looking to find a problem that wasn't really there. She decided to change the subject.

'Oh - I meant to check something with you,' she said. 'My friend Eve's back from London in a couple of days and I was going to ask the girls up here for a book club meeting one evening if that's okay with you?'

'I forgot you mentioned that you're in a book club,' he said, surprised. 'Somehow I just can't imagine it!'

'Well, it's quite an unusual book club,' she grinned. 'We *do* read a book - and we talk about it for, maybe, a minute or two. Then we drink wine and set the world to rights.'

'Sound like my kind of book club!' he laughed.

'I was thinking it would be a really good chance for me and Sue to rope the rest of them in to help with the fayre. Lucy runs the pub, Emmy's got Grandad Jim's Flower Farm, Eve is an incredible artist and Caro owns the Vintage and Upcycle shop in the craft centre. That's a lot of possible stalls, or workshops, or at the very least - raffle gifts!'

'Then do it!' Will nodded.

'Cool. We'll probably take over the living room if you don't mind?'

'Course I don't!' he laughed.

'Well, just thought I'd better check with the boss,' she grinned.

'I thought we'd agreed to drop that.'

'Sorry,' said Amber with a smile. He really was proving very easy to tease.

'Just . . . maybe don't tell them all about the weddings yet? I know Sue already knows, but maybe not the rest of them for now? I'd hate that rumour to spread if Horace decides he doesn't want to do it after all.'

'Fair enough,' said Amber, though she couldn't help

AUTUMN CUDDLES AND MUDDY PUDDLES

but feel a bit gutted - she'd been looking forward to showing off their ideas for the library - especially to Emmy. She could only imagine her friend would go absolutely wild to fill that room with flowers. 'Do you think he *will* go for the idea in the end?' she asked, reluctantly bending over to wrap her hands around her end of the trough.

'I hope so!' said Will, puffing a bit as he lifted his side. 'It would bring in good money, be a sustainable income for the hall, and it wouldn't take too much to get going. I'm just not sure Horace can *see* it yet if you know what I mean? He's too attached to the image of the library as his - what did you call it - *man cave?*'

She nodded and they both fell silent for a moment as they puffed and dragged the trough into position.

'Don't they make lighter versions of these?!' gasped Will.

Amber nodded as they carefully set it down next to the other one. 'They do - but I didn't want to spend money when I already had these down at the craft centre!'

'That's my girl!' grinned Will, then he promptly blushed bright red and looked at his feet. 'Sorry. Inappropriate comments of our time proudly present . . .!'

Amber couldn't help but smile and she reached out to pat his arm. 'I'll let you off!'

'Just don't tell Sue,' he muttered. 'She'll think I'm trying to corrupt you or something.'

Amber sniggered. 'It's not up to Sue who gets to

corrupt me.' Then she paused, mildly horrified that had actually come out of her mouth. 'Ahem,' she added.

'Quite,' muttered Will, sending a grin at her that was half delight, half horror. 'Want a hand getting that willow in to soak?'

'Erm, okay. I'll get these filled if you could cut the ties on that first bundle?'

Amber unrolled the hose and positioned the nozzle inside the first trough. She headed back over to the standpipe and cranked the tap on full, only to be met with a high-pitched squeal.

She span around to find the hosepipe wriggling like a demented snake. The end had jumped clean out of the trough and had given Will a thorough soaking with freezing cold water.

Amber started to laugh as she watched him trying to pin it down, only to get the jet straight in the face.

'Turn it off, turn it off!' he spluttered.

It was no use, Amber was now laughing so hard she was bent double with her hands resting on her knees for support, tears pouring down her face as she watched him chase the end in erratic circles. The lawn was getting muddier by the second, and Will was completely drenched.

By the time he managed to pin it down, Amber was gasping for breath, clutching at her sides.

'Thanks for your *help!*' he spluttered, making his way back towards the trough.

'Sorry, but you were . . . just . . . so . . .' Amber

erupted with laughter again, waving her hands over her head in an imitation of Will's epic muppet-flail as he'd tried to catch the wriggling hosepipe.

'Right,' said Will, abruptly changing direction.

'Oh no!' squealed Amber. 'No, no, no nooooo!'

Will ran straight for her and wrapping one arm around her, he promptly held the end of the hose directly over her head like a shower.

Amber let out a yelp as the cold water cascaded over her scalp and then poured straight down the back of her neck.

Trying to wriggle out of his grip, she stretched up and managed to aim the torrent back at him for a few seconds. Will yet out a yell - but neither of them was able to get away from the gushing water for long as they both had a hand on the pipe, fighting for control.

'Truce! Truce!' Amber spluttered as the jet hit her again. She relinquished her grip on the hose, screwed up her face and tried to rub the water out of her eyes.

'Okay,' laughed Will, throwing it away from him so that it landed neatly in the trough behind them.

Amber ran her hands down her face, flicking a slick of water from her skin and then grinned up at Will. He was standing so close to her that she could see droplets glistening on his eyelashes. His hair was dripping onto his cheeks, forming little rivulets that traced the contours of his face.

Without thinking, she raised her hand and gently stroked them away with her fingertips.

Will stood completely still, staring at her in surprise, seemingly frozen to the spot.

What was she doing? This was Will. Slightly grumpy, slightly annoying. Will - her manager. And she was still Amber - who didn't want anything in her life to change, who loved things exactly the way they were, and who definitely didn't want a relationship that might dictate how she had to live her life. But right now? Right now, none of that mattered.

She trailed her fingers across his damp skin towards his lips, moving so slowly it was as though the entire world had almost stopped turning. Even Will's breathing seemed to have slowed.

Amber leaned forward. He was taller than she'd realised. She stretched up, closing the space between them until her damp lips met his in the most barely-there kiss she could manage while standing on her tiptoes in the middle of a muddy puddle.

The entire world seemed to pause as the warmth of this tiniest of contacts radiated through her body. All the sounds and colours of the beautiful autumn day faded into the background as Will wrapped his arms around her, pulling her so close that their sodden jumpers squished together. He deepened the kiss and she wound her arms around his neck, twining her fingers into his wet hair.

It was the sound of rushing water that finally broke through their little bubble and forced Amber back into the real world. She twisted around in Will's embrace to find that the first trough was overflowing.

'Oopsy!' she said lightly. 'Better swap that over!' She drew away from Will and quickly sloshed the end of the hose into the second container. Now that the contact between them was broken, she wasn't sure what to do.

She turned and couldn't help but smile. Will hadn't budged an inch - he was just watching her with a slightly dazed expression on his face.

'You okay?' she asked, crossing her arms in an attempt to warm up a bit. She was suddenly very aware that she was soaked to the skin.

Will simply nodded. 'You're shivering!' he said, taking a step towards her. Then he paused, clearly realising that he couldn't exactly offer her an extra layer as he was just as drenched as she was.

'Nothing that can't be fixed by a change of clothes and . . . a hot chocolate?' she said.

'Now you're talking!'

'Here - give me a hand with these quickly, and we'll go inside,' said Amber, switching into practical mode so that they could get the willow on to soak before they both went down with hypothermia. Whatever had just happened between them - well, it would just have to wait. She couldn't examine what it meant until she was warm, dry and preferably within sipping distance of a gallon of hot chocolate and whipped cream.

She grabbed a bundle of withies, separating them from the rest, and added them to the first tank.

'How many do we need to put in?' said Will, following suit.

'All of them,' said Amber with a grin.

CHAPTER 10

'Okay - I have to say, this place really suits you,' said Caro from her perch directly in front of the roaring open fire.

'Ha - yeah, right,' laughed Amber. 'I'm not sure I was designed to play lady of the manor - I'm not really dignified enough.'

'Rubbish!' said Lucy from the depths of her corner of the sofa. 'I'm with Caro - this place is definitely doing *something* for you - you seem more . . . chilled? Maybe that's the wrong word. You seem even more *you* than usual.'

Amber snorted and took a sip of wine.

'I've got a theory,' said Eve.

'Here we go - it's pile on Amber time!' laughed Amber.

'No, hear me out!' smiled Eve. 'My theory is that it's

not Bamton Hall that suits Amber so much - but someone *at* the hall.'

Damn and blast Eve and her ability to cut right to the crux of the matter as usual. Amber opened her mouth to argue, and then promptly shut it again as she felt the heat of a blush start to rise to her face. She couldn't really argue, could she? Eve was right, but she was buggered if she was going to give up that particular bit of gossip so soon in the evening. She needed a hell of a lot more Dutch courage before that happened - especially with Sue in attendance.

'Yep - you're right,' she grinned. 'I love having the dogs around. Tarmac and Diesel complete me,' she sighed theatrically, placing her glass on the mantelpiece and making a heart shape with her thumbs and index fingers.

'Give over,' giggled Emmy from her armchair. 'These two horrors?'

The two horrors in question were sharing the hearth rug with Caro and were currently being as good as gold. Both of them were stretched out on their sides, as close to the fireplace as they could manage without actually getting singed.

'In case you haven't noticed, they're reformed characters,' said Amber in mock indignance.

'Actually,' said Lucy, sitting forward, 'I was going to ask you about that. Have you got them drugged or something?'

'Yes,' said Amber. 'Overdosed on fresh air and exer-

AUTUMN CUDDLES AND MUDDY PUDDLES

cise - and we're giving them less of those processed treats Horace got them hooked on - I swear the pair of them were just high on the doggy version of sugar all the time!'

'So you're telling me they're trained and well behaved now?' said Emmy, raising her eyebrows sceptically.

'Ha! Fat chance,' laughed Amber. 'But at least they don't try to chew your shoes while they're still on your feet anymore!

'Right,' said Sue, 'I hate to change the subject, but I think it's high time we turned our attention to the important business of the evening!'

'Moonfleet?' said Caro, stroking the book that was sitting on the rug next to her.

'No, dozy,' laughed Sue. 'I want to know what Amber's been getting up to with the new boy?'

'Excuse me?!' spluttered Amber. 'I haven't been *getting up* to anything.'

'Don't give us that,' said Lucy, rubbing her hands together. 'For one thing, you've got your guilty face on, and for another . . . Violet said something about the pair of you - and a *hose?!* Though, to be fair, I might have misheard her.'

'God, this village is *unbelievable* sometimes,' sighed Amber. 'But . . . you didn't mishear her.'

Caro squealed. 'You two'll have such beautiful babies!'

'Caro, love,' said Amber, holding up a hand, 'I'm

sorry, but enough with the whole baby obsession, I'm begging you.'

Caro stuck her bottom lip out and pretended to pout.

'Well - Caro does have a point,' grinned Eve.

'Right - that's it. One more mention of babies and I'm not giving you any gossip.'

'Oh - I wanna know!' wailed Lucy. 'Gimmie the gossip! We haven't had anything decent since Eve seduced Finn and had her wicked way with our very own favourite author!'

'Oi!' said Eve, blushing. 'Besides - not true. What about Alf's sciatica?'

'Eve, no one counts poor Alf's sciatica as juicy gossip,' laughed Emmy. 'Not even Alf! Come on Amber - spill!'

'It's not a big deal.'

'Answer us this,' said Caro. 'Did it involve a man?'

Amber nodded.

'Was there *touching?*' Caro continued, wiggling her eyebrows.

Amber nodded again, then jumped as Caro, Lucy, Eve and Emmy let out a round of simultaneous, high-pitched squeals that made the dogs both jump to their feet. Sue simply leaned back in her chair and crossed her arms, looking stony-faced.

'Then it's a huge deal,' said Caro, beaming at her, and stroking both the dogs at once in an attempt to make up for frightening them. 'I've never known you to be interested in - well - *anyone!*'

'That's because I *haven't* been interested in anyone,' muttered Amber. 'And anyway - who said I was interested?'

'Stop stalling and give us the juicy details,' demanded Lucy.

'Fine. Will lost control of the hose, he got soaked, I laughed at him, he soaked me, we kissed, the end.'

All five of them stared at her blankly for a moment before the giggling started.

'Thank goodness you're not a writer,' spluttered Emmy. 'That has to be the least romantic description of a first kiss I've ever heard.'

Amber swallowed. Tough. That was all they were going to get out of her. She wasn't even sure she could explain to *herself* the way the kiss had made her feel, let alone this bunch of piss-takers. The way time seemed to have slowed. The way she could still see the water droplets clinging to Will's eyelashes whenever she closed her eyes. The way his lips had felt when she'd brushed them with her own.

'You okay?' said Sue, still watching her.

Amber nodded.

'Was it that bad?' asked Eve gently.

'Bad?' said Amber in surprise, then shook her head. 'No. At least, I don't think it was. It wasn't for me . . . it was . . . well, it was a couple of days ago, and neither of us has even mentioned it since. We just finished the job, came back inside, got dry, had a hot chocolate to warm up and - well, that was that.'

'Who initiated it?' asked Caro.

'Erm - me,' said Amber, feeling slightly embarrassed. 'I mean I didn't pounce on the poor guy or anything, but . . . oh God, do you think I *pounced* on him?!'

Lucy shook her head, looking concerned. 'Course you didn't. It sounds like you were both being playful and one thing led to another and-'

'How much do you know about him?' demanded Sue.

Amber shrugged. 'Not masses. He seems like a decent guy. Has a stubborn streak, but don't we all?'

'No - I mean about his background - his personal life. Does he have a wife? A girlfriend?'

'Sue!' squeaked Lucy.

'You don't think . . .'

Caro was shaking her head. 'Course he doesn't. He wouldn't have kissed you otherwise!'

'I thought we just ascertained that *she* kissed *him*!' said Sue.

'I'm starting to feel like I'm on trial here, guys,' muttered Amber.

Caro reached over and patted Amber's hand, but Amber abruptly moved away to add a log to the fire, not wanting the contact while she was feeling so on edge. She hated this!

There *had* been something in that moment with

Will that had made her feel really uncomfortable - not because it shouldn't have happened, but because she was shocked at how much she *wanted* it to happen. Even worse was how desperate she was for it to happen again.

She tossed the log into the fireplace and grabbed the poker to push it into the perfect spot.

'Actually,' she said, turning back to Sue, 'I've just remembered that Will mentioned an ex on our first day up here . . .' Amber tailed off.

She didn't want to tell them all the next bit she remembered - that he'd sworn off family and relationships. That he just wanted to focus on his work and nothing else. Shit - had she misread the entire moment and just bulldozed him into something he didn't want? Sure, he'd wrapped his arms around her, kissed her back - but that could have just been a physical reaction to the moment, couldn't it?

That said, if anyone had asked her about whether she was looking for a relationship when she'd arrived at Bamton Hall, she would have echoed Will's thoughts almost exactly - minus the ex of course. She definitely hadn't been interested in finding someone, or in kissing the most gorgeous man she'd ever met. Now it was practically the only thing she could think about.

'Yeah,' she said again, clearing her throat. 'He has an ex he's doing his best to avoid by being here. He's not in a relationship.' She huffed out a breath. She could really do with someone changing the subject now.

'What about kids?' said Sue.

'Oh for heaven's sakes!' said Lucy, walloping Sue with a cushion.

'What? It's a fair question.'

Amber shrugged. 'I don't know. I don't think so.'

Even as she said it, the memory of how great he'd been with Belle and Richie came back to her. The reality was, she simply didn't know anything about William Jones. Other than the fact that she really, *really* wanted to kiss him again.

'Look,' said Sue, 'all I'm saying is - get to know a bit about the guy.'

Amber shrugged, Sue had a fair point. 'What's your problem with him?' she said.

Sue looked surprised, and a slightly nervous glance seemed to make the rounds between the others.

'Sorry,' said Amber. 'That came out way more bluntly than I meant, but-'

'It's fine,' said Sue, holding her hand up in a conciliatory gesture. 'I just don't want to see you get hurt, that's all.'

'But why would he hurt me?'

'Just . . . you don't know him,' she said.

Amber frowned. 'But we don't really know anyone when we first meet them, do we? It's a process, right?'

'Me and Lucy knew each other for years,' said Sue.

'You two are special,' said Amber with a small smile.

'Amen to that,' said Lucy with a huge grin, snuggling into Sue's shoulder.

'But . . . that doesn't answer my question. You've had a problem with Will since the moment you met him!'

'You would too if you'd tried Googling him!' muttered Sue.

'You didn't?' gasped Eve, staring at her.

'Might have,' said Sue, swirling her wine around in her glass for a moment.

'And?'

'I think you should look for yourself. Check out the kind of work he's done in the past.'

'What was he,' laughed Caro, 'an international hitman?!'

Sue sighed. 'Look, I'm just not sure about his motives for being here at Bamton Hall, that's all - for taking this job.'

'Why not?' demanded Amber, folding her arms. She was starting to feel pretty cross now, but she wasn't sure if it was at Sue for stirring up a can of worms, or at herself for how much she wanted to jump in and defend Will.

'Okay, look,' said Sue, 'his last company had something to do with buying and selling properties. Large properties. Like this one.'

'So what?' said Amber. 'He was made redundant. He's used to managing big projects, and problem-solving, and saving money. Everything that's needed here.'

'But what if he's not really here working for Horace? What if he's here to soften him up, ready to sell the place? Maybe this is his way of getting his job back ... or ... auditioning for a new company!'

'Don't be ridiculous,' laughed Amber.

'Amber's right. Why would he do that?' said Eve. 'It sounds like Horace has known him a really long time. He wouldn't have him here if he didn't trust him.'

'Plus, from what Amber's told us, he's come up with some great ideas - like the fayre,' said Emmy.

'And he's been supportive of Amber's work, hasn't he?' said Caro.

Amber nodded. She so badly wanted to get off this topic before her head exploded. She usually loved nothing more than hanging out with this amazing bunch of women, but right now she needed a nice, peaceful room where she could lie down - preferably in the dark - and take a few deep breaths.

Sod Will's orders to remain shtum about holding weddings at Bamton Hall. He was the one causing all this discomfort, so he could damn well provide the distraction she needed.

'Yeah,' she said, 'Will's been full of amazing ideas - and the best one has to be turning the West Wing into a wedding venue!'

'What?!' demanded Lucy. 'Oh my goodness, that's so exciting - this would be the most magical place to get married!'

Perfect. The excited squeals from her friends were just what she'd been hoping for. With any luck, that would put an end to the Will-bashing for one evening.

'Look,' she added, 'this is all top secret until Horace agrees to it, okay - so you guys have to promise to keep quiet?'

'Of course we will!' said Eve, her eyes twinkling.

'Then let's go to the library,' said Amber, urging everyone to their feet, then linking arms with Emmy. 'I want to hear how you'd transform the room for someone's big day.'

CHAPTER 11

'I meant to ask, did you have a good time with your book club the other night?' said Will, as they strode across Bamton Hall's front lawn, leaving tracks in the thick frost that had arrived overnight.

The two dogs trotted in wide circles around the pair of them as they all headed over towards the sculpture of The Huntress, which was just starting to take shape.

Even though it was only the long skirts that were fully woven so far, Amber felt a pang of pride as the graceful curve of the sculpture emerged between the trees. It was going to look really special when it was completed.

'We had a great time, thanks,' said Amber with a smile, watching her breath plume in the cold, morning air. She pulled her jacket more tightly around herself. 'So, did you feel much discomfort around the ears?'

'Huh?' said Will, looking confused.

'I can only imagine they were burning. Thoroughly!!' she smirked.

He glanced at her, looking a bit pink, though that might just be the cold air working its magic.

'Oh yeah?' he smiled. 'Care to fill me in on the gossip?'

Amber could have kicked herself. Why had she even mentioned it? After all, she didn't really want him to know that she'd told them all about their one and only kiss - not least because it was looking increasingly like that had been a random, one-off thing, never to be revisited. And she *definitely* couldn't tell him that he'd been the subject of Sue's sudden and even more random attempt at amateur sleuthing.

'Oh, you know - just about the fayre, and how things are going here, and . . . stuff.'

'Stuff? Right,' said Will, and she was relieved to see that he was still smiling. 'Well, you and Sue did a great job of roping the others into helping at the fayre. They've been really generous.'

'Yeah. See, I told you they would be. Oh, and Sue said it looks like she'll be able to borrow a bunch of marquees for us from the local vineyard, so that'll save us a drenching if it decides to rain. Anyway, what do you think?' she said, pointing towards the half-completed sculpture.

Will stared for a few moments then turned and grinned at her. 'It's going to be beautiful. I can't wait to see the finished thing. I . . .' he stopped and cleared his throat awkwardly. 'Actually, I should come clean about something.'

Amber's heart squeezed. Uh oh, that sounded ominous.

'Don't look so worried,' laughed Will. 'It's just that I looked up the work you did on that RHS garden.'

'Oh,' said Amber with a rush of relief. 'The cart-horse!'

Will nodded. 'I mean - he was amazing. No wonder you guys won gold.'

'I'm under no illusions that was just because of my input,' she laughed. 'Those designers were amazing to work with. Bit of a dream come true for me, that project. Not unlike this one.'

'Well, you can't really compare Bamton Hall to winning gold at Chelsea, can you?'

Amber nodded. 'I totally can. It's not often you get to create an entire trail of permanent sculptures. Add to that the living willow structures that are going to be here long after I'm gone. I mean, working in a landscape I love so much - it's a . . .' she trailed off, searching for the right words.

'Dream?' said Will, smiling.

Amber shrugged. 'Well yes, it is! Little Bamton and this whole area is *home* for me. No matter where I end up, it'll always be home. This project means I'm leaving something behind me - and hopefully, it'll be enjoyed by generations to come.'

Will looked up at the sculpture then back to her again. 'I get it - that feeling of wanting to make a positive, lasting difference to something you hold dear.'

'Exactly,' she said, nodding.

'Speaking of future generations,' said Will, as they wandered across the stretch of lawn that he'd earmarked for the fayre, 'may I remind you that you made a promise to invite two of them up here!'

Amber glanced at him in surprise. 'You mean Belle and Richie?'

'Of course!' said Will. 'Richie was so excited to help you, and if you don't follow through on your promise of a princess sleepover, I doubt very much that Belle will ever forgive you!'

'You're right,' said Amber.

She suddenly felt awful. She'd been so busy helping to get all these mad plans for the fayre in place - not to mention that she'd been pretty preoccupied with obsessing over what might or might not be happening with Will - that her promise to the kids had almost slipped her mind. It was so unlike her that she could kick herself.

'How come you're so good with kids?' she asked.

Will shrugged. 'I've got a niece and nephew I adore. They moved away a couple of years ago and it nearly broke my heart not being able to see them as much. We still video-chat all the time, but it's not the same.'

Amber nodded, her heart squeezing as Will frowned.

'Sorry,' she said, 'that must be really hard. I've only known these two for about three years and I cried my eyes out the day I moved up here.'

'I can understand that!' said Will gently.

'It's weird,' said Amber, 'I never really thought of myself as a child-friendly person.' They skirted around the various spray-painted outlines that were just about visible through the frost, each one representing a stall they were hoping to fill. 'Actually, I've never given much thought to having kids of my own, but those two-'

'Got under your skin?' said Will.

'Exactly.'

'Yeah, same for me. I don't think it's about being "child-friendly", I think it's just like falling in love. You fall for that individual - that special person,' he paused and looked her right in the eye, 'and everything that makes them so completely unique,' he added in a low tone.

Amber swallowed, suddenly unsure whether they were still on the topic of kids or if they'd moved on to something even more ... problematic.

'So,' said Amber, breaking eye contact with him and deciding to quickly change the subject - a skill she was becoming ridiculously good at, 'Lucy's agreed to run the bar,' she pointed at a long oblong outline, 'Emmy's going to have a flower stall and do a couple of autumn wreath-making workshops, Caro's going to bring her badge-making kit, Sue and the guys at the allotments are going to have a local produce stall, Violet's got the local WI rounded up to run a cake and jam stall, Eve's going to hold a silent auction of about a dozen of her paintings . . .' Amber stopped to take a breath. 'Who've I forgotten?' she said.

'Alf and Thor are going to do cart rides,' said Will, 'the guys down at the garage are going to bring their pedal go-karts up and set up a racetrack around the lower paddock as long as we can get the grass cut in time, and *you're* going to bring stock up from your unit to sell, and run some kind of workshop too?'

Amber nodded. 'Wow - sounds pretty good, right?'

'And then there's Violet's idea of a Halloween costume parade, and apparently, Horace is friends with someone who does sock-puppet shows.'

Amber laughed. 'Of *course* he is! So - do you think we're going to be ready in time?'

Will paused and sucked in a deep breath. 'Yup,' he said decidedly. 'We're going to be ready. As long as you can finish your two sculptures in time?'

Amber nodded. 'No issues there. And you've managed to sort out the insurance?'

Will nodded. 'We've got a guy coming tomorrow to check out the trees on the drive and the two oaks here next to where the fayre is going to be. The rest will have to wait until we're ready to look at opening things up further.'

'So, fingers crossed they're all safe?' said Amber.

Will nodded. 'Exactly. If not, we'll need to rope someone in to do the work super-fast.'

'Things are going to be so full-on until the fayre's over, I'm not sure when I'm going to have the chance to get the kids up here,' said Amber, looking worried.

'Aren't they off school at the moment?'

Amber nodded. 'Long half term or something.'

'Then why not call Mia and see if her and Ben fancy the night off tonight? If they're anything like my brother and his wife, they'll take your arm off!'

'Tonight?' said Amber in surprise.

'Sure, why not?'

'But - I haven't got anything ready for them.'

'If you fancy, I can knock up pizza dough and we can all have that for tea? It's going to be a beautiful day, so Richie can work with you out here and I can help keep Belle amused, then we'll stuff our faces and watch a Disney movie together?'

'Disney? Really?' said Amber with a smirk.

'What says "princess" better than Disney? And I know for a fact there's a good selection in Horace's DVD collection because I spotted them the other night when I was looking for something to watch to take my mind off... stuff.'

Stuff? Amber raised her eyebrows but decided not to comment. 'Question is - will that be "princess" enough?' she said, raising her eyebrows.

'We'll make crowns!' laughed Will.

'Okay,' she said, 'as long as you're sure you're up for helping?'

'If there's one thing I've learned as an uncle, it's that if you make a promise to kids, you've got to keep it.'

'Well, as long as you don't mind . . .'

'Mind?' laughed Will, leading the way back towards the house, 'I can't wait for a double-bill of Aladdin and Beauty and the Beast!'

'Thanks Will,' she said. 'I'll give Mia a call and see what she thinks.'

∽

'Amber! Amber! Look how many leaves me and Will got. Look at the colour of this one!'

Amber turned to watch Belle scuttling towards her at a rate of knots, the little woven basket she'd given her bouncing along the ground.

'Wow Belly, look how red that one is!' said Amber.

'See Richie, see!' said Belle, holding the bright red maple leaf up in front of her brother's nose for him to inspect.

'Nice,' said Richie. Then he passed two withies from the pile next to him over to Amber and watched closely as she deftly wove them into the waistline of The Huntress.

'Tell your brother what we're going to do with them, Belle,' said Will, finally catching up, puffing slightly as he came to a halt and ruffled Belle's hair.

'We's going to make strings of them for the party!' said Belle.

'Cool!' said Richie.

'Party?' said Amber.

'She means the fayre,' grinned Will. 'We can all have a go when we're watching films later!' he added.

Amber cast a quick glance in Will's direction to check that he wasn't totally knackered from running around after the energetic five-year-old for the past hour. Catching her eye, he winked at her and she did her best to ignore the butterflies that took flight in her stomach.

As Will had predicted, Mia had jumped at the chance of a rare child-free day, so Amber and Will decided to make a quick raid on the nearest supermarket. After loading up with plenty of pizza toppings, hot chocolate supplies and assorted treats, they'd driven back to Little Bamton to collect an over-excited Belle and a slightly more laid-back Richie from their exhausted and ridiculously grateful parents - who promised to collect them the next morning.

'How're you guys getting on?' asked Will, coming closer to watch Amber work for a few seconds. 'Wow! You've done loads.'

Amber paused. 'Well, I speed up loads when I've got Richie to help me, don't I mate?!'

Richie looked chuffed, but he shrugged.

'Looks like you know exactly what you're doing,' said Will, impressed.

'I've been helping for years,' said Richie, passing another two withies to Amber.

'Yup. Richie knows exactly what I need to be handed even before I do. Saves soooo much time!'

'Wow!' said Will.

'I help too!' said Belle, scampering forward and tugging at Will's trouser leg, making him laugh.

'Yeah - you help make a mess, don't you Belly?' said Richie.

'A great big mess,' said Belle, nodding her head solemnly, making the other three laugh.

'Right princess,' said Will, 'I think we need to leave these two in peace to work for a bit longer?'

He aimed the question at Amber, and she nodded back, mouthing a subtle "yes please!"

'But I wanna help,' said Belle, bending down and aiming to pick up one of the withies.

'Well, maybe we can go and make crowns for all of us to wear tonight?'

'Yay!' said Belle, instantly springing back up and grabbing Will by the hand. 'Bye Richie. I'll make you a big crown for your big head!'

'Er, great, thanks,' he laughed

CHAPTER 12

Amber knew that she was in serious danger. That's why she'd left Richie and Will gossiping together while they loaded the dishwasher with the breakfast things. She couldn't believe it - it was like the pair of them had known each other for years, and Richie's monosyllabic answers were nowhere to be seen. In fact, she'd barely been able to get a word in edgeways. Not that she minded, it was the perfect excuse to take a sleepy Belle out for a wander in the gardens and get her own head on straight. Mr William Jones had her all of a dither, and if she wasn't very careful, she was going to pounce on the poor guy again.

The previous evening had been wonderful. The four of them had giggled their way through three Disney movies together, the lads gamely wearing their "crowns" that Belle had made for them - basically four sticks held together by a bunch of string. Will got top marks for enthusiasm, but not so much when it came to crafting skills!

With her belly full of homemade "princess" pizza, followed by trifle and hot chocolate, Belle had conked out in Amber's lap, and eventually Will had carried her upstairs to one of the camp beds they'd set up in Amber's room. Richie had followed, promptly declaring it the "best day ever".

Then there had been the awkward moment when Will had gone to kiss Amber on the cheek and she, like the numbnuts she was, hadn't noticed and turned just in time to get a kiss right on the mouth. This had prompted a decidedly impressive wolf-whistle from Richie, while the two of them blushed bright red, giggled nervously and made several comments along the lines of *gosh, is that the time?!* all while staring at the floor.

After Will had excused himself with a backwards glance at Amber that was full of something - it *might* have been longing, but it might simply have been too much pizza and hot chocolate - Richie had had a good laugh and hooted "awkward!" before flopping down under his borrowed blankets.

Awkward was just about right. Both of them had been using the kids as buffers during breakfast, determinedly not looking at each other for too long. Amber sighed and sucked in a lungful of crisp autumn air. That was the thing though - apart from that accidental kiss - the evening before had been anything *but* awkward.

Looking after the kids with Will had felt completely natural - and the image of him gently carrying a sleeping Belle upstairs in his arms seemed to be seared into her brain. It was doing something very funny to her insides. Yup - she was definitely in serious danger when it came to Will - and she wasn't sure if she should be feeling excited or terrified.

'Can we pick up more pretty leaves?' said Belle, grabbing Amber's hand and pointing over to the small group of young maples at the far end of the garden.

'Sure, Belly!' said Amber.

'Can you carry me?' said Belle, letting out a huge yawn.

Amber chuckled and hoisted the little girl up in her arms. 'Come on then.'

'I can't wait for the party,' Belle sighed in her ear.

'I know,' said Amber, 'it's going to be brilliant.'

'Do you think Will will make us more pizza then?'

Amber laughed. 'I'm not sure. Maybe if you ask him nicely! But I think there's going to be chips and hot dogs and burgers and all sorts.'

'Not as good as Will's pizza,' she said stoutly.

'I'll tell him you're a fan. Right - here we go - grab those leaves!'

She plonked her back down and Belle instantly started sorting through the mat of vibrant reds and yellows. Amber was sure there was some kind of selection process at work, but for the life of her she couldn't figure out what made Belle toss some leaves away while others were lovingly shoved into her duffle coat pocket.

She made a mental note to warn Mia that she was sending her daughter home with half a compost heap in her coat pockets.

Amber was just rubbing her hands together, trying to get a bit of warmth into them, when she caught a movement out of the corner of her eye. Spinning around, she came face to face with two people she'd never set eyes on before. They looked quite bizarre against the backdrop of the early-morning gardens, dressed as they were in formal suits, the woman struggling slightly on blocky high heels. Amber blinked a couple of times, wondering if she was seeing things.

'Morning!' said the man, as they both made their way over towards her.

'Erm, hi!' said Amber. 'Belle, lovely, come here a minute.'

Belle toddled towards her and turned to stare at the two strangers.

'This one's for you,' said Belle, and with a grin, she pulled out a crumpled leaf and presented it to the suited man. He raised a pair of bushy grey eyebrows before taking it from her on auto-pilot.

'Thank you, young lady!' he said, straightening back up, a surprised smile appearing on his face.

'I'm a princess,' said Belle.

Amber put her hand on Belle's head protectively.

'Sorry,' she said, smiling at them politely. 'I didn't know we had any visitors here this morning.' *Especially not this early in the morning*, she added to herself.

'I'm Elaine Harries, and this is my colleague, Rhys Johnson,' she said as if that was going to explain everything. 'We were told to have a look around whenever we were passing - I hope that's okay?'

'Oh,' said Amber, 'of course it is.'

It wasn't really up to her, after all. There were so many people involved in getting things at the hall up and running - from tree specialists, to council members, to health and safety officers - that she'd rather lost track of who was going to be around and when. These two definitely had the whiff of health and safety officers about them.

'I don't suppose Will Jones is around, is he?' said Rhys.

'He's looking after my brother!' piped up Belle.

'Not to worry,' he laughed, 'we'll catch up with him next time.'

'Here's our card,' said Elaine, handing one over to Amber from her pocket.

'Can I have one?' asked Belle, taking an eager step towards Elaine, who promptly took a step back.

'Here Belle, you hold this one for me,' said Amber, quickly passing her the card without looking at it.

'Fanks!'

'Right, well,' said Rhys, 'we'd better leave you two to your morning walk.'

Amber nodded and smiled back politely. She wasn't sure what they were trying to achieve, but one thing was for sure, having Belle there to "help" wasn't going to speed things up for them.

'Nice to meet you,' she said, turning back towards the house as Belle waved at the pair of them. After a few moments, Amber looked over her shoulder just in time to see them turn onto the path that led around the back of the hall. 'Well,' she said quietly, 'that was weird.'

'What's this word?' said Belle, who was busy peering at the business card in her hand.

Amber smiled and knelt down next to her to take a look.

'Hotel,' said Amber in a small voice as a massive block of ice slid into her stomach. 'That word is hotel.'

~

Amber stood stiffly at Will's side on the drive as he waved back at the kids, who were busy pulling faces at the pair of them through Mia's car's rear window. She felt like everything was happening through some kind of weird fog - getting Belle back to the house, making sure her and Richie had both packed all their things and then trouping them outside to meet their mum.

'Thank you both so much!' said Mia, turning to

them after fighting to buckle Belle into place. 'It was so nice to have a quiet evening together.'

Amber just nodded and didn't say anything. She knew it wasn't fair on Mia, but she couldn't trust herself to open her mouth right now.

Will glanced at her, then realising she wasn't going to say anything, jumped in. 'We had a blast, didn't we?' he said, nudging her arm.

Amber nodded again and forced a smile onto her face. Mia raised an eyebrow at Amber and then swooped in for a hug.

'You okay?' she muttered in her ear, under the cover of the cuddle.

'Tell you later,' breathed Amber.

Mia pulled back and stared at her for a second before opening her arms out to Will. 'I've got a feeling I'm going to be hearing an awful lot about you over the next few days, Will,' she laughed.

Will raised his eyebrows and shot a worried glance at Amber, making Mia snort. 'I meant from the kids. You've definitely earned yourself a couple of super-fans there!'

'It's the pizza,' he said with a smile and a shrug. 'Always a winner. And for the record - they're really great kids.'

'Thanks,' said Mia, looking chuffed, 'we think so.'

'Isn't Ben waiting for you?' said Amber, trying to keep her voice light and failing miserably.

Mia nodded. 'Yeah. Better go.'

The pair of them waved as the car pulled away down the drive, and then Amber turned and strode back towards the hall without saying a word to Will.

'Hey - what's up?' he called, following hot on her heels. 'Have you had an argument with Mia or something?'

'With Mia?' she squeaked, stopping so abruptly that he nearly ploughed straight into the back of her. 'Of course not.'

'Well then, what's with all the rude-vibes back there? You practically kicked her off the estate!'

'If I did, it's because I didn't want her to witness the real argument that's about to happen!'

'Real argument . . . what the hell?' said Will, looking surprised. 'I thought we just had an amazing evening together. Did I do something wrong with the kids, or-?'

'No,' said Amber, 'you were perfect with the kids. Amazing.'

So amazing that you nearly had me fooled!

'So what's the problem? I thought we were getting on . . . more than getting on. I thought-'

'Whatever you thought, you can forget it!' she spat. 'I can't have anything to do with someone I can't trust.'

'I don't know what you're going on about, but that's pretty rich coming from you!'

'Excuse me?!' spluttered Amber.

'I had a message from Lucy this morning asking me about weddings up here at the hall - apparently, she'd like to know more.'

Amber's mouth dropped open. She had no idea what Lucy was up to, but right now wasn't the time to worry about it.

'So?' she said defensively.

'So you told her!'

'Did you consider that maybe it was Sue who blabbed, not me?!'

Will frowned at her. 'Was it?'

Amber blew out an annoyed breath and scuffed her shoe into the gravel. 'Fine - no - it was me!'

'I asked you not to share that with them all!'

'I just wanted them to know how hard you were working to save this place,' she said, her voice rising. 'Or at least I *thought* that's what you were doing!'

'Of course that's what I'm doing - that's why I'm here, isn't it?!' he said, looking confused.

'Well,' said Amber, reaching into her pocket, her fingers closing around the little square of card that had given his game away, 'this says otherwise!' She slapped the business card hard into his chest.

Will fumbled, dropped the card and then slowly bent down to pick it out of the gravel. He quickly scanned the words. 'Where did you get this?' he asked quietly.

'This morning. In the gardens. They were here to "look around!"' she said. 'And don't tell me you've never heard of them - they asked for you by name!'

'Of course I've heard of them,' he said. 'Everyone who's worked in my industry has heard of the Sunrise

Hotel Group. They own most of the manor house hotels in the South West. My old company used to do business with them all the time - they even offered me a job at one point. But I have absolutely *no idea* what they were doing here.'

'Yeah, right,' said Amber, doing her best to ignore the fact that he looked completely thrown. There was no way she was going to fall for his bullshit again. Sue's instincts about him had been right - he must have been planning something with these people right from the word go. She'd fallen for a front - a version of him that wasn't even real.

'Look,' said Will, pocketing the card, 'whatever this is, it isn't important right now. We've got work to do, a fayre to run-'

'Oh my God,' said Amber, her mind racing, 'this is why you wanted to keep everything so secret at the beginning, isn't it? You knew none of the projects up here would actually happen because you'd have already done your deal. Bamton Hall's going to be sold and turned into a frickin' hotel, isn't it?!'

'Don't be ridiculous,' snapped Will. 'I just wanted to make sure I got everything right before going public with our plans. Horace has put a lot of faith in me - I needed to prove myself!'

'Bollocks,' said Amber.

'It's the truth. But then *you* taught me that it was better to be open with the local community - that they'd want to be a part of our future here - that they'd want to help!'

'Yeah - and that's turned out to be the perfect distraction, hasn't it? Keep us all focused on the fayre while you've been doing your little deal with Rhys and Elaine?'

'You're talking out of your a-'

'Was this your plan from the start?' she cut across him. 'Did you come here just to convince Horace to sell Bamton Hall?'

'I would never-' spluttered Will

'I don't believe you. Why make nice with the kids? Why kiss me? Was that all just part of the distraction too?!'

'How dare you?' he growled.

Amber stepped back, breathing hard. She knew she shouldn't have said that. She was lashing out because she was trying so desperately hard not to cry. How could she have been so wrong about him?

But what if you're not wrong? What if this is all a misunderstanding?

Amber shook her head. She couldn't think about that, because if she *was* wrong about Will being involved, she'd basically just hammered the last nail into the coffin of any relationship they could have had.

'I love kids,' he said quietly, 'and those two are adorable - and, well, they're important to you, so-'

'Yeah, so?' said Amber.

'So - I just really enjoyed hanging out with them. And you.' Will took a step towards her.

Part of Amber wanted nothing more than to reach out to him, take his hand and apologise. Instead, she crossed her arms protectively across her chest. She wasn't going to let him trick her again. She'd been too wrapped up in him to notice that something had been going on right under her nose.

'You kissed *me*,' he said quietly, looking down into her eyes. There was a note of pleading in his voice.

'Not that it matters now, but we kissed each other,' she said.

'Yes. I guess we did.' Will sighed, his eyes flicking down to her lips.

For just a second, Amber thought he was going to lean in and kiss her again. Instead, he closed his eyes briefly before turning his back on her.

'So - all this?' she said. 'Everything we've been doing?'

'All this is what it's going to take to save this place!' he said, turning back to face her. 'Whatever's going on with Sunrise, it's nothing to do with me. You have to believe me!'

Amber shook her head. 'But I don't,' she said quietly.

'Well,' said Will, looking at her sadly, 'then there's nothing more to say to each other. I'm proud of what I've done here.'

'Yeah - you're nearly there, aren't you?' she said, her

voice hard as she desperately tried to cover the fact that something inside her had just shattered. 'You've nearly got what you want,'

'Yes,' sighed Will, locking eyes with her for a couple of seconds that seem to stretch on for hours, 'I nearly got what I wanted. Looks like that's over now though, doesn't it?' he added, before turning and walking away from her.

CHAPTER 13

'Alright, what's with you?' demanded Emmy.

'With me?' asked Amber, tearing her eyes away from Will, who was busy humping straw bales off the back of a quad bike and setting them out as seating in one of the three giant marquees they'd already managed to set up.

'Yes you, misery guts,' said Lucy, holding on firmly to one of the legs of the final marquee - the one they were still fighting with.

'Nothing, I'm totally fine,' lied Amber, forcing a smile onto her face.

'Ha!' laughed Sue. 'You're not fooling anyone.'

'I'm good, it's just been full-on,' she said, glancing quickly over towards Will to check that he was occupied. 'Talk in a bit?!' she muttered in a low voice, jerking her head in Will's direction.

'Oh right, got ya!' said Lucy quietly, raising her eyebrows.

'Oh dear,' said Emmy, looking worried.

'Alright then ladies, let's get this piss-ant of a job finished,' said Sue. 'On three!'

'Three!' yelled Amber

Gripping a leg each, the four of them shuffled awkwardly backwards away from each other

'And ... stop!' yelled Sue.

'God I hate these things,' muttered Emmy, eyeing the half-erected marquee with dislike and sucking her finger where she'd just managed to pinch it.

'I know,' said Amber, 'but I thought they'd be a good idea. It *is* October after all, and we don't want a classic Devon downpour or two to spoil the fayre after all this work!'

'It's good thinking,' said Sue. 'Plus it means everyone can set up their stuff in advance, so that'll make things a bit calmer on the day!

'Well - thank you for getting them for us!' said Amber gratefully. 'They cost a fortune to hire.'

'Yeah - the only drawback is having to put the buggers up ourselves,' muttered Sue. 'Alright. Here we go. Let's get the legs up to the halfway point!'

～

'Never again,' said Emmy.

With much swearing, they'd managed to get the metal frame with its canvas roof all the way up. Now Caro and Eve were adding the wind and waterproof sides - with much muttering as they fought with the strong Velcro tabs as they tried to get them lined up correctly.

'I can't thank you guys enough,' sighed Amber, stretching her back.

'So,' said Sue, watching Will zoom off on the quad bike to collect more straw bales, 'what's going on? You two've barely looked at each other this morning, let alone talked to each other!'

'Yeah,' said Caro, straightening up from securing the last tab and linking arms with Amber, looking exhausted. 'We were expecting a luuuuuurve update!'

Amber flinched and automatically checked over her shoulder to see who else might be in hearing distance. It was just the six of them - Violet and Horace were over the other side of the lawn, setting up trestle tables inside the largest marquee.

'Come see my sculptures,' she said loudly, indicating for them to follow her even further away. There was no way she wanted to let the cat out of the bag by mistake. 'I've finished The Huntress, and I should have the wild boar done this afternoon.'

They all gathered around the flowing skirts of The Huntress, and her friends looked up with their mouths open.

'Okay, Amber,' said Eve. 'I know you're an expert

and medal winner and everything, but *this* is something else!'

Amber cracked a genuine smile for a split second before the look of pure misery she'd been wearing since her fight with Will quickly replaced it.

'Alright, enough,' muttered Sue. 'What's up?'

'You were right,' whispered Amber, and the others instinctively drew nearer so that they could hear her better. 'I found two random strangers wandering around the garden the other morning. When I asked who they were, they gave me a card.'

'And?' prompted Lucy.

'And they're from a massive hotel chain.'

'No!' breathed Emmy.

'Yep.'

'I don't get it,' said Eve, 'how does that make Sue right?'

'It makes her right about Will,' said Amber. 'That he's been up to something dodgy ever since he got here.'

Eve shook her head. 'No, it doesn't. It just means there were two people from a hotel chain up here looking around. It doesn't mean it's got anything to do with Will!'

Amber shrugged. 'They asked for him by name. Anyway, who else would have asked them up here?'

'But - what were they doing here?' said Emmy.

'Scoping the place out, I guess, ready to swoop in on Horace as soon as Will's managed to soften him up.

Then they'll turn it into some awful boutique hotel. I bet they're hoping for a bargain price too if Will's told them that Horace is struggling.'

'Did you ask Will about it?' said Caro.

Amber nodded. 'Oh yes. We had one hell of a bust-up and basically haven't spoken since.'

'He admitted that's what's going on? That it was him who invited them?' asked Emmy in surprise.

'He said he knows the company,' said Amber, 'but denied all knowledge as to why they were here.'

'Well then!' said Eve. 'If he said he didn't know—'

'It *had* to be him!' said Amber, only just holding back from stamping her foot. It *had* to be him, otherwise she'd made one of the biggest mistakes of her life, accusing him like that.

'Well, it certainly does look like it,' said Sue. 'What did poor old Horace say?'

'I erm . . . I haven't told him yet!'

'Why not?! demanded Sue. 'Amber - this is urgent!'

Amber shook her head. 'I don't really know how to tell him to be honest. Plus, I've thought about it and I reckon it's best to keep quiet until after the fayre is over. If there's a big bust-up now then the fayre might not happen, and that would just mess everything up.'

'Love,' said Lucy, wrapping her arm around Amber's shoulders, 'I hate to say it, but if there's a big company like that sniffing around, I think there's a good chance everything's pretty messed up already.'

'You're probably right,' sighed Amber. 'But part of

me just really wants to pretend none of this is happening. The fayre will still make some money for the Church Fund - so at least it means all our work won't be completely wasted.' She paused and dug the toe of her boot into the ground, trying to get control over her quivering chin. 'It'll be a good send-off for the old place. But I'm going to need to look for somewhere else to live as soon as it's over. Whatever happens, I can't stay here now.'

'Honestly,' said Eve gently, 'I think you're jumping way ahead of yourself here. Why would Will have started pushing plans to turn the West Wing into a wedding venue? Why do so much to organise the fayre? Why would he have supported you with the sculpture trail? None of it makes sense - not if he was just planning on getting Horace to sell the place!'

'That's true,' said Caro. 'And why would he have started something with you, Amber?'

Amber clenched her jaw. Damn her stupid wobbling chin! She cleared her throat, determined to get her words out. 'I think it's all been about distraction. Keep us all occupied elsewhere - tied up with other stuff - while he was busy screwing us all over.'

'I'm so sorry,' said Sue, shaking her head.

'Yeah. Me too,' said Amber.

'But . . . I still think we should tell Horace,' said Sue.

'Actually, love,' said Lucy, looking thoughtfully at Sue, 'I'm with Amber on that one. The fayre's only a few days away. Let everyone enjoy it without this news hanging over their heads. It'll be good for Horace to have the entire village up here, lending him their support.'

Emmy nodded. 'It might give him the boost he needs too - you know, for when he has to deal with it all. He needs to know that Little Bamton's on his side, no matter what he decides to do!'

'Well, I don't like it,' muttered Sue, crossing her arms and glaring across the lawn towards Will, who'd just returned on the quad bike.

∼

Amber was knackered. What was it her mother used to call it? Bone tired, that was it. Today had really taken it out of her - and in any normal circumstances, she'd be chilling out with a glass of wine and toasting herself to a day's work well done. Instead, she was huddled under her duvet watching Beauty and the Beast on her old laptop while cradling a long-cold cup of tea.

Between them, they'd got everything in place for the fayre - now all they needed were the stallholders with their goodies, some decent weather - and the entire village to turn up and bring the place to life.

On top of everything else they'd achieved today, Amber had also managed to finish off her wild boar sculpture. It had been the perfect excuse to avoid having anything to do with Will after the girls had gone. She was genuinely chuffed with how it had turned out, but the achievement felt more than a little bitter-sweet now that she knew she might not get the opportunity to finish the rest of the trail.

Amber let out a huge sigh. She was done for, but it wasn't just the physical work that had left her feeling so hollowed out. She hated to admit it, but it had been a huge relief when her friends had called it a day and headed home.

After dropping the bombshell about Will and Sunrise Hotels, Amber had spent the rest of the day on high alert, worrying that Sue would take matters into her own hands and punch Will's lights out. She hadn't, of course, but the added anxiety had just about finished her off.

At least one thing had become very clear to her as she'd worked on the boar - she really *would* need to find somewhere else to live. The sooner the better. Even if Will didn't succeed in his plans and Horace decided not to sell Bamton Hall, there was no way she could remain living here if Will was going to be here too. If Horace saw sense and chucked him out on his ear for what he'd done, she'd still have to leave - because there was no way she could stay when every second at the hall would remind her of what had almost happened between them.

Even if their time together had just been some kind of weird, twisted way to keep her distracted from what was really going on, she'd still managed to lose a part of her heart to Will - or at least - to the version of him who was great with kids, loved Disney movies, and made the best pizza she'd ever tasted.

Amber sank down a bit further into her pillows, blinking hard against the tears that had been threatening to fall all day.

'Shit,' she sighed, rubbing her eyes hard. All she really wanted to do right now was bawl her eyes out and then curl up and go to sleep. It was only half-past six in the evening, but it wasn't as if anyone would know...

A sharp knock at her bedroom door made Amber jump and slosh cold tea down her front and across her keyboard.

'Damn!' she muttered, hitting pause on her laptop while desperately trying to mop the tea up with her sleeve. 'One sec!'

She shoved her duvet aside, hopped out of bed and shuffled over to the door on slippered feet.

'Erm - who is it?' she asked lightly. She didn't want to fling it open only to find an angry Will ready for battle - not when she was wearing a tea-stained Snoopy sweatshirt and a pair of slightly baggy leggings.

'Just me,' came the cryptic reply.

Amber frowned. 'Horace?'

'Yep. I can go away and come back later if this isn't a good time?'

'It's fine,' said Amber, opening the door and forcing a smile. 'Do you want to come in?'

He nodded. 'If you don't mind? Don't worry, the boys are down in the library!'

'Come on in,' she said, stepping out of his way and swiping her rucksack off the armchair so that he could sit down. She half wished that he'd brought the dogs too - she could have done with the distraction.

'Look, I'm sorry to turn up at your door unannounced. I know it's a bit random, but I wanted to talk in private.'

'It's fine,' said Amber. 'Is everything okay?'

'Everything is fine with me, but I suspect that's not the case for you?'

'What makes you say that?' said Amber, sinking down onto the foot of her bed, a sense of doom settling in the pit of her stomach. Was she going to have to tell him everything after all?

'Well,' said Horace, tearing his eyes away from the tea stain on her sweatshirt and smiling at her gently, 'it doesn't take a genius to know that something has gone decidedly awry between you and Will.'

'I-'

'No point arguing!' he said, holding up his hand. 'I'm far too old - and Violet's far too wise - to miss something that obvious. And we both agree that it's a terrible shame - especially when everything looked so promising between you after that little water fight!'

Amber let out a mortified squeak, making Horace chuckle. 'I was young once too, you know.'

'But I'm not-'

'What did I say about arguing?' said Horace, doing his best to look stern.

'Sorry,' she muttered.

Horace sighed. 'Look. Sue came to see me earlier.'

'Damn and blast that interfering woman!' said Amber.

'Now, don't be too hard on her - I don't want you blaming Sue for any of this. She just went into protective-mother-hen mode - for me, and the hall, and you too. You know what she's like!'

Amber nodded, doing her best not to grind her teeth.

'Look, if you want to blame anyone, blame me!'

'But I don't blame you!' said Amber in surprise. 'You must be in bits - finding out that Will has gone behind your back and-'

Horace shook his head. 'You misunderstand me. I was the one who invited Elaine and Rhys from Sunrise here for a visit. It was ages ago and besides, I never dreamed they'd turn up so early in the morning!'

'You?'

'Yes. Me. Not Will.'

'But when I found them in the garden, they asked for Will. And when I spoke to him about it, he said he'd heard of the company. I just thought - I just . . . oh no!'

'You thought there was some kind of skulduggery afoot?'

Amber nodded as all the awful accusations she'd hurled at Will started to replay in her mind.

'I know I should have told you both that I'd asked them here, but the simple truth of the matter is - I'd forgotten all about it - there's been so much going on!'

'Really?' said Amber, struggling to catch up.

'Yes!' said Horace. 'Look, it *was* Will who introduced me to their company to start with.'

'Then he *has* been trying to get you to sell the hall?!'

'No!' said Horace. 'Amber, sweetheart, you need to give that boy a break! He's had a hard time of it.' Horace let out a sigh. 'I'm guessing he hasn't told you much about himself?'

Amber shook her head.

'No,' said Horace. 'Well, he's proud - that's been half the problem. Will loves to work - and he puts his heart and soul into whatever job he's doing.'

'Yeah,' muttered Amber. 'I've noticed that.'

'Did he tell you he was made redundant from his last job?'

Amber nodded.

'What I'm sure he *didn't* tell you is that Lois, his witch of a fiancé, ditched him the minute that happened. *Because* it happened, in fact.'

'What?! Oh God, poor Will,' said Amber in surprise.

'Yes, you could say that. She told him that she'd only consider taking him back if he found himself a new position - but it had to be a better one with more money.'

'Who *does* that?!'

'Someone who doesn't deserve to spend their life with Will,' growled Horace.

Amber watched as he took a long, deep breath, clearly trying to calm down.

'Like I said, Will's proud,' he said at last. 'Losing so much, and then accepting a job from me - his dad's best friend - well, let's just say I think he felt like I was offering him charity. I really wasn't - I needed him here. His skills are just what Bamton Hall needs. But, well, I think he feels that he has rather a lot to prove.'

'Right, but I don't get what this has got to do with Sunrise Hotels?' said Amber.

'Before I offered him the job here, Sunrise tried to headhunt Will. They'd worked out via the grapevine that there was this long-standing connection between the two of us. So, they approached Will and offered him a deal - if he could convince me to sell Bamton Hall to them, they'd make him Head of Acquisitions.' Horace paused. 'Of course, with that job he'd stand a very good chance of winning Lois back!'

'What?!' shrieked Amber.

Horace held up his hand. 'Will drove straight here and told me all about it. He turned them down.'

'He did?' said Amber.

Horace nodded. 'That's when I decided to make him an offer of my own. He'd already proven that he was loyal to a fault. Will told me that if selling up was something I ever wanted to consider, he'd help me through it, but I wanted him to show me what my other options were - what could be done to save this place.'

'But then what were the guys from Sunrise doing here?'

Horace shrugged. 'I didn't think it would hurt to hear what they had to offer. Again - don't mistake me - I would *never* sell Bamton Hall to them after the way they attempted to go about things, but I decided I'd like to know what kind of money I'd be looking at if we failed and I did need to sell.'

'And you didn't tell Will about this?'

Horace shook his head. 'I wanted him focused on saving the place, not selling it.

'I just wish . . . I wish I'd known.' said Amber shaking her head. 'I gave Will such a hard time, and he was so angry!'

'Of course he was - but more with me than you, I think. Until you told him that Rhys and Elaine had been here, he had no idea any of this was still going on,' sighed Horace.

Amber nodded, finally understanding. 'So, it was as much a shock to him as to me . . . and there I was ranting at him!' said Amber, her eyes wide with horror. 'He's worked so hard . . . we've *both* worked so hard!'

'I know you have!' said Horace. 'Amber - I've been struggling for a while now, but coming back from France to hear all these amazing plans the two of you have cooked up - well, it's just confirmed that there's plenty more we can do here. Seeing how much the village is behind me has made me realise that what I really want is to stay here at the hall and turn it into something special. But I can only do that if I've got you two to help me!'

Horace leaned forward and took Amber's hand. 'I know Sue said you were looking to leave, and I understand. But the question is, now that you know everything, will you accept my apology for doing this all the wrong way around? For not telling you everything? Are you willing to stay? I need you to finish the sculpture trail and work with Will to bring Bamton Hall back to life.'

Amber swallowed hard and nodded. 'Of course. But only if Will's okay with that too.'

'Well . . . I'm not going to pretend that he's not angry,' sighed Horace.

'Oh God, I'm so sorry-'

'Not with you, girl - with me! After being so straight with me, he expected - and deserved - the same in return, and I failed him. I've apologised of course, but he's gone to stay with his mum for the night. I think he needs to cool down a bit - but I *hope* he'll forgive me and pick up where he left off.'

'I'm sure he will,' said Amber, squeezing Horace's hand. 'I really need to apologise to him for jumping to conclusions. I should have *known* he'd never do anything like this, but Sue . . .'

'Sue feels awful for putting ideas in your head!' sighed Horace. 'She was only-'

'Trying to help,' said Amber, with a rueful smile.

Horace nodded.

'I wouldn't blame Will if he never wants anything to do with me again,' said Amber, 'but I've got to try! Do you think I should I call him?'

Horace shook his head. 'If you want my advice, I think this is one of those things that you need to do face-to-face. I'd let him have this evening to cool off. Besides, you could do with getting a good sleep too, by the look of you. Talk to him when he gets back tomorrow evening, when you're feeling . . .' he glanced down at the giant tea stain on her top again, 'erm, fresh?'

Amber pulled a face. 'You're right.'

'Good. Excellent. Now that we've got all that ironed out, there's one more thing I need your help with before I leave you in peace?'

'Go on . . .' said Amber.

'This whole idea of holding weddings at Bamton Hall . . . do you really think anyone would be interested?'

CHAPTER 14

Amber paced around her little studio in the craft centre. She was nervous and waiting for Emmy to arrive wasn't helping. She took a deep breath and let it out slowly, looking around her space. It had been weird not being in here very much recently, but Emmy had done a lovely job of combining Amber's willow pieces with her own wonderful displays of both fresh and dried flowers. It gave her confidence that if anyone could help her with today's insane mission, it was Emmy.

Amber had ended up talking to Horace about weddings at Bamton Hall for well over an hour the previous evening, and in the end, he'd agreed that if she could *show* him that the library would make the perfect venue, then he would give Will's plan the go-ahead.

'No pressure,' muttered Amber to herself, peering through the windows as she waited. The minute

Horace had left her on her own, Amber had got straight on the phone to Emmy and the pair of them had concocted a plan. In Amber's head, the success of this plan was now completely tied up with whether she and Will were going to manage to sort things out or not.

'Right! I'm here and ready to roll!' said Emmy, bowling into the studio and making Amber jump. 'Oops, sorry!' she laughed. 'I thought you'd seen me.'

Amber shook her head and chuckled. 'I was looking straight at you, but my head was . . . somewhere else!'

'With Will?' said Emmy, striding around the space and gathering various tools and bits and pieces and shoving them into a tote bag.

'Yeah.'

'Well, all of today's flowers are ready and waiting to be loaded onto the back of the land rover once we've got what we need here.'

'*All* your flowers? But your stall-'

'Don't argue - if we can win Horace over and I get to do the flowers for the weddings at the hall - then it's going to be worth it, right?'

Amber raised her eyebrows. 'Erm yeah - you're absolutely right!'

'So, it's an investment. And anyway, I'm excited about transforming the library with you. Even if Horace doesn't decide to go ahead with the plan, I'm bringing my camera and I'll use this in my portfolio and on social media!'

'Good idea! It's going to be a lot of work, do you reckon we'll get it all done in time?' asked Amber. 'I've asked Horace if he can keep Tarmac and Diesel out of there for us - they're so much better these days, but I didn't think they'd be particularly helpful considering most of our work is about de-dogging the room!'

'Good thinking!' said Emmy. 'And don't worry, we'll get it done in time. We'll make sure of that. Now then, which one of these arches were you thinking of taking up with us?' she asked, turning to the three sweeping willow arches that were currently set against the walls of the studio.

'Which one would be best for you in terms of adding flowers?' said Amber.

Emmy considered them for a moment and then pointed at the two on either side of the room. 'Either of these because they are wider and so have got more space to show off the wood and the flowers without either getting overwhelmed. And as we're going for an autumn theme, they've both got that bit sweeping across the top that'll be perfect for suspending leaves from.'

'Then let's go for this one,' said Amber. 'It's my absolute favourite, and it's a bit taller than the other one. Plus it echoes the shape of the arched window in the library.'

'Right - let's get it loaded into the back of the Landy, fetch the flowers and make a start!'

~

They'd just pulled carefully onto the driveway of Bamton Hall so as not to upset the buckets of flowers packed into the back when Emmy turned to Amber with a worried look on her face.

'What's up?' said Amber, casting her a quick glance.

'I think I should come clean about something.'

'Uh oh, that sounds ominous,' laughed Amber. 'What is it about this week and secrets?'

'Well . . . I *might* have roped in a little bit of extra help today to make sure we get everything done.'

'Oh lord, what have you done . . .?'

Amber pulled up outside the hall right next to Sue's truck. Well, that saved Emmy answering the question, didn't it?!

'Don't be mad,' said Emmy. 'Sue was in bits by the time she'd finished with Horace yesterday. She told us she'd got it all wrong. Apparently, it was as much as Horace could do to stop her coming to find you straight away.'

'I'm glad she didn't,' muttered Amber. 'I don't think I'd have been very welcoming.' She hopped out of the Land Rover, slammed the door and headed around the back.

'Well, no,' said Emmy, catching up with her. 'Horace told her he needed time to explain everything to you and that you'd probably need a bit of time to cool off.'

Amber nodded. That pretty much echoed his advice to her about Will.

'Look, she just wants to make everything up to you.'

'We'll see,' said Amber.

Emmy cast her a nervous glance, but Amber didn't trust herself to say anything else, so she grabbed a bucket of flowers in each hand and made her way towards the side door to let them both in.

Emmy followed about a step behind her all the way down the hallway, neither of them making a sound on the carpeted floorboards. Amber had the distinct feeling that Emmy was deliberately staying just behind her, not wanting to be the first one into the room.

Pausing at the closed library door, Amber set her buckets down.

'Give me a sec,' she said, turning to Emmy.

Emmy nodded, still looking worried. Amber felt bad, but she simply wasn't sure what was about to happen and really didn't want her to get caught in the middle of it all.

She turned the handle and quietly pushed the door open, only to be met with a roar of sound.

'AMBER'S HERE!'

Before she could figure out what was happening, Belle, closely followed by Richie, pelted straight into her, wrapping their arms around her.

'Oi, you two!' called Mia, from over by the window.

Amber hugged them back and then stared, open-mouthed as she watched Mia wring out the rag she was using to sluice down the filthy windows, then wipe her hands on a nearby towel.

'Hello lovely!' said Lucy, who was on her hands and knees, sweeping up the old ash out of the fireplace and emptying it into a galvanised bucket.

Amber couldn't wrap her head around what she was looking at. Caro was over in the corner, wiping down ancient books and then placing them one by one back onto the newly cleaned shelves. Eve and Sue looked like they'd just been interrupted in the middle of shifting the heavy desk towards the back of the room, and Violet was pouring cups of tea for everyone out of a huge brown pot over on a table in the corner.

'We's come to help you,' said Belle, giving her a squeeze. 'But mum said Will isn't going to make pizza today,' she added, sticking her bottom lip out.

Amber couldn't help it, she let out a little laugh before turning to look enquiringly at Emmy who was still hovering behind her.

Emmy shrugged. 'You needed help. I did what we always do in Little Bamton - called in the cavalry!'

Amber nodded, smiled at her, then looked around again, trying to take everything in. The room had already started to transform, and a little bubble of excitement formed in her stomach. If they could pull this off and convince Horace before Will returned that evening, then it really would mean a new start for Bamton Hall.

As Amber looked from the newly-gleaming

windows over to the almost empty fireplace, Sue caught her eye. She seemed to be frozen in place, a half apologetic, half terrified look on her face.

For the briefest moment, a tingle of annoyance went through Amber. If it hadn't been for Sue's unfounded warnings about Will, she might never have jumped to the conclusions she had. But then the smallest quiver of Sue's lip melted her heart. This was her friend, and she'd only been trying to protect the people she loved.

'Come on guys,' muttered Amber, bending low to talk to the two kids, 'time to pounce on Sue!' and, straightening up, the three of them bounded across the room and gathered Sue in the middle of three-way group cuddle.

'I'm so sorry,' Sue half sobbed, half laughed in Amber's ear as the pair of them stood with their arms wrapped around each other. The kids on the other side of her were creating a kind of huggy-Sue-sandwich.

Amber pulled back a little bit so that she could look her friend in the eye. 'Don't worry about it.'

'I shouldn't have-'

'It's forgotten.'

'All this change just got me worried. It's only because I care-'

'I know,' said Amber firmly. 'I get it!'

Sue nodded, but Amber could feel that she was still wound up like a spring.

'I'll apologise to Will, of course. Poor bloke.'

'Yeah, well . . . that's something I've got to do too,' sighed Amber. 'But I reckon, if we can pull this off today, it'll be a damn good start, right?'

Sue nodded, and visibly pulled herself together. 'Thanks Amber. Seriously.'

Amber shrugged. 'We're friends.'

'And friends do weird things sometimes!' snorted Sue.

'Ain't that the truth?' laughed Amber, giving Sue a final squeeze.

'Right you lot!' called Violet. 'There's tea here for everyone.'

'And biscuits?' asked Belle, instantly scuttling over to Violet's side.

'And biscuits,' laughed Violet, stroking the little girl's head.

'Hey Caro,' said Lucy as she passed the desk that Eve and Sue had left abandoned in the middle of the floor, give me a hand with this a sec?'

Caro looked at Lucy and shook her head. 'I can't.'

'It's not too bad,' said Lucy, lifting one end, testing the weight.

Caro shook her head again, 'Sorry, I-'

'I've got it,' said Sue, leaving Amber's side and, hurrying over to take the other end of the desk, she and Lucy lifted it out of the way into the corner.

'You okay?' said Amber, joining Caro.

'Oh, I'm fine . . . I . . .'

Violet lifted her eyebrows and Amber noticed a definite gleam in her eyes as she looked at Caro.

'Well,' said Caro, as everyone gathered around the table and helped themselves to a cup of tea, 'I guess I'd better tell you all. I'm pregnant.'

There was complete silence for all of two seconds before the library erupted in cheers of delight and Caro was swamped by hugs from all sides.

'Does Sam know?' said Lucy, with her arm still around Caro's shoulders.

'Of course,' laughed Caro, taking a sip of tea and then beaming around. 'He's so excited! I'm sorry to spring it on you like this, but he's asked me to move up to the cabin with him.'

'Of course he has,' said Lucy, looking delighted. 'Oh my, your own little family. This is such lovely news! And there's your problem solved too Amber! If you still need to move, you can have the flat over the pub.'

'She's not going anywhere,' puffed Violet.

'Well - if I can't work things out with Will, I might have to,' said Amber sadly.

'Surely it won't come to that,' said Sue, looking horrified.

'I'll finish the work for Horace of course,' said Amber, 'but it might be better if I wasn't living on site - it wouldn't be fair to Will! Besides, if today's plan goes well, you'll need my room back as a guest bedroom! Anyway - let's not worry about all that right now - I want to know more about this baby!' she said, turning back to Caro.

Caro shrugged, still beaming. 'Nothing much to tell. We've decided to leave the sex a mystery, I've had a bit of morning sickness, but not too bad, and I've suddenly got a bit of a thing for oranges, but I hate marmite!'

'Well, it's wonderful news,' said Violet. 'I'll have to start knitting.'

'I keep thinking - this little bean's so lucky,' said Caro, gently stroking her stomach, 'it's got an entire village to love it!'

'I can vouch for that being the very best way to bring up a kid,' said Eve with a grin.

'Also, I'm sorry I've been a bit baby obsessed,' laughed Caro, turning to Amber. 'At least now you know why!'

'It all suddenly makes sense,' said Emmy with a chuckle.

'My mummy's having a baby too!' said Belle, patting a bemused Mia gently on the stomach. 'And I helped paint the nursey!'

'Nur-ser-y,' corrected Richie, rolling his eyes and helping himself to another gingernut. 'And for the record, I helped paint over Belle's bits.'

'So how are you feeling?' asked Lucy, looking at Caro.

'Excited. Scared. Nervous - then excited again,' she laughed.

'If you need any advice, or just need someone to

talk to,' said Mia, smiling gently at her and stroking Belle's head lovingly, 'I've had a bit of practice. I'm right here, just shout.'

'Same,' said Eve nodding. 'Davy might have been eighteen years ago, but still . . . I've been there, done that and most definitely got the tee-shirt!'

'Thanks guys,' said Caro.

'All right everyone,' said Violet, draining her cup, 'we'd better get back to work. We've got a fake wedding to prepare by lunchtime!'

CHAPTER 15

A knock at the door at exactly half-past twelve sent them all scurrying.

'Are you ready yet?' boomed Horace's voice from outside.

'Give me two seconds!' yelled Emmy, quickly trimming the last few stems on the arch, then grabbing her reel of floral tape off the floor and shoving it in her pocket before turning to Amber.

'Have we forgotten anything?' she hissed.

Amber peered around the room, and even though she'd been here all morning working alongside her friends to transform the filthy, doggy man-cave into what it was now, it still managed to take her breath away.

The willow archway they'd set up in front of the window framed the stunning view out across the gardens. It seemed to invite the autumnal colours of the trees right into the room, where they were echoed in the newly scrubbed and polished wooden floor which now glowed with the warmth of beeswax and elbow grease.

The arch itself was woven with a profusion of flowers, grasses and autumn leaves. The jewel tones of the dahlias Emmy had used seemed to glow against the rich velvet of the leaves Richie and Belle had helped her to string up.

They had filled the open fireplace with five ornate candle holders, each adorned with matching leaves and flowers and bearing a stout church candle. They'd even used the leaf garlands the kids had made with Will on their princess sleepover to weave around their bases, covering the blackened stone.

'Eve,' said Amber, who was sitting nearest the fireplace, 'can you light the candles, I forgot!'

Eve gave her the thumbs up, quickly knelt down and grabbed the lighter they'd left there ready for the job.

'Everyone ready?' asked Emmy, turning to the others.

There were smiles and thumbs up from around the rest of the room. They'd decided that, to give Horace the full experience, it would be fun for him to walk down the aisle. In order to do this, they'd pilfered every chair they could find in the West Wing and set them out in rows, facing the willow arch. Emmy had even gone so far as to hang a little floral arrangement on the backs of the ones nearest the aisle.

'Alright kids,' said Amber, 'you ready for your part?'

Belle nodded excitedly, and Richie shrugged.

'Close enough,' she laughed and took her place under the arch to welcome Horace in. Emmy took her seat next to Eve while Belle and Richie made their way to the back of the library to open the door for Horace.

Amber watched as he took one step into the room and drew to a crashing halt, his mouth dropping open.

Richie, who'd been holding the door open, quietly closed it behind Horace, and then Belle, whose job it was to scatter autumn leaves and petals down the aisle in front of him as they walked, looked up at him and frowned.

'It's okay, Howace! Hold my hand and I'll take you to Amber.'

She thrust her little hand into his, and Horace smiled down at her as he let her lead him towards the front. Once they reached Amber, Belle dropped his hand and then quickly ran back towards the door, emptying her basket in great big handfuls as she went, making the others laugh.

'You did all this?' he said, looking all around him - taking in the beautiful floor, the archway overhead and the flickering candles in the fireplace. 'Today?'

'We did,' said Amber very quietly. 'I couldn't have done this without my . . . erm . . . congregation?' she grinned.

Horace peered around at the others and did a double-take. 'Goodness - I didn't know we had house-elves!' he laughed.

'Like in Harry Potter!' squeaked Belle from her mum's lap, where she'd retreated after she'd finished emptying her basket.

'So,' said Amber, 'what do you think?'

'Lots of things!' said Horace, looking around him again like he still couldn't quite believe his eyes. 'For one thing, my two horrors are going to have to get used to sleeping in the old butler's room - I'm not letting them back in here!'

Amber nodded and chuckled. *Thank heavens for that!*

'For another thing - I can finally see what Will was talking about. This really would be a magical place to get married . . . don't you think?' he said, turning to look at Violet.

'Don't you go getting ideas, Horace!' laughed Violet.

Horace winked at her and then turned back to Amber. 'In answer to your question though - do I want to turn part of Bamton Hall into somewhere people can pledge to spend the rest of their lives together? It's a yes. Or in these circumstances, maybe I should say - I do?'

'Yay!' squealed Amber, and she threw her arms around Horace and gave him a massive hug as the others all cheered. 'So, erm . . . when do you reckon you'll tell Will? As soon as he gets back?'

Horace shook his head. 'Oh no, this isn't my bit of

news to share, I'll leave that up to you. After all, you've both got lots to talk about anyway, so what's one more bit of news?' he said, looking decidedly mischievous.

'Are you sure?' said Amber. 'If we can't work things out between us, you won't want plans for the hall affected!'

Horace shook his head. 'I've got complete faith that the pair of you *will* work everything out!'

'So what's the plan?' asked Violet, as everyone joined them under the arch.

'Well,' said Horace, 'I'd suggest you do exactly the same with Will as you did with me. It's quite the eye-opener. Only . . . maybe try it without the congregation next time,' he laughed.

Amber grinned, but the knot of nerves that had been hovering in her stomach all day tightened at the idea.

'Blimey,' laughed Sue, 'he's going to think you're proposing to him!'

'You don't think it'll scare him off?' said Amber, now feeling totally freaked.

Mia took her hand and squeezed it. 'It won't.'

'But what if-?'

'Amber,' said Sue gently, '*if* it does, then let's just say that he's not made of strong enough stuff to be with you.'

Amber swallowed and nodded, even though the thought of it made her chest feel tight.

'Somehow, though,' added Sue, 'I've got the feeling he might just be spot on.'

～

If she thought she'd been nervous earlier, waiting to see if they could convince Horace that the grand wedding plan was a good idea, it was nothing compared to how she was feeling right now.

Amber was on her own in the library, waiting for Will to arrive. Violet had stuck her head around the door about five minutes previously to warn her that he was back on the estate, and since then she'd been nervously pacing under the arch, running over and over in her mind what she wanted to say.

She wished that the dogs weren't banned from the room. Right now, a hug from Diesel and Tarmac was just what she needed to stop her hands from shaking. That said, she still didn't trust their newly-discovered good behaviour enough to let them anywhere near the beautifully decorated room - not when there was so much riding on it - and especially not when the candles were still flickering in the fireplace. She wanted them to be dowsed later with the fancy candle-snuffer that Horace had produced, not the cock of a naughty Labrador's hind leg.

After much discussion, her band of "helpers" had decided that it would be best if they all headed back down to the village, rather than getting involved. This had produced a full-on protest from Belle, who'd had her heart set on leading Will down the aisle just as she had with Horace.

Belle's tears almost made Amber change her mind, but she was glad now that she'd stuck to her guns. She was having a hard enough time keeping herself calm, and besides, it might feel a bit like she was trying to manipulate him with excess cuteness if Belle was around - she knew he couldn't say no to the little monkey - and as much as she'd love to use that to her advantage right now, it simply wouldn't be fair. It had been Richie who'd come to the rescue, telling Belle that he was sure they'd both get to hang out with Will at the fayre. Amber made a mental note to treat Richie to several free rides on the go-karts.

Amber had just started to fiddle with the leaves hanging from the back of the archway when a light knock at the door made her turn

Horace's face appeared and he raised his eyebrows at her. She nodded and he disappeared again.

'Horace,' came Will's voice as he came into the room looking backwards over his shoulder, 'can't we do this later? I could really do with . . . oh!'

He'd just turned fully into the room and spotted Amber, waiting for him under the archway.

'What's going on?' he breathed, his eyes darting around the room and a look of confusion crossing his face.

'I'll - um - I'll leave you both to it,' said Horace,

shooting a smile at Amber and quickly retreating, closing the door behind him.

'Amber?' said Will, turning back to her, his eyebrows raised in confusion.

Amber stared at him, and for just a second it felt like everything she wanted to say to him was stuck in her throat, all the words caught up in a strange ball of emotion as she looked at him.

'This *is* the library, right?' Will said, looking around him again without taking another step.

Amber watched his eyes run along the mismatched rows of chairs, scan the candles in the fireplace and then travel back to the stunning archway before coming to rest on her again. She nodded. 'Yes. It's the library. I . . . we . . . we thought we'd try out your idea for it,' she said lamely.

'You did all this today?' said Will.

Amber shrugged. 'With a little bit of help from our friends . . . and two very enthusiastic small people,' she added with a tiny smile.

'It's . . . well, it looks incredible, but-'

'Will, I'm so sorry,' said Amber, unable to keep her apology to herself for a minute longer. 'I'm sorry I accused you, sorry I didn't listen to your side of things . . . sorry I even thought that you might do that,' she said, all her thoughts coming out in a jumble.

She took a couple of steps towards Will and then stopped, not really knowing what to do. She wanted to take his hands, beg his forgiveness and hug him. But

Will was standing there with his hands in his jeans pockets - staring at her with a frown on his face - looking more than a little bit alarming.

'Look, I shouldn't have listened to Sue. And I shouldn't have even thought that you'd . . . that you'd . . .' she trailed off again. Crap, this wasn't going how she'd planned at all. They weren't going to manage to fix this, were they? And it was all her fault. She couldn't blame him. He needed someone who trusted him, and she'd proven herself to be the exact opposite. And now, she couldn't even manage to apologise properly.

'Sue texted me,' he said at last.

Amber raised her eyebrows in surprise. Of all the things she thought he might come out with, that wasn't the one she'd been expecting.

'She wanted to apologise and didn't want to wait,' his eyebrow gave a tiny quirk of amusement. 'Bit of a character trait, I suspect?'

Amber nodded. 'You could say that,' she said quietly. 'Her heart's in the right place,' she added.

'Look, I'm sorry too,' he sighed, taking his hands out of his pockets and running them through his hair. 'I should have been more open with you. Things in my life have just been spectacularly crap recently, and it's made me a bit . . . guarded?'

'You don't need to explain,' said Amber.

'But I do. I owe you that,' he said.

'Horace told me some of it,' said Amber quickly, wanting to be open with him now, if nothing else. 'And he told me you didn't know anything about Sunrise turning up.'

Will shrugged. 'So, erm, what's all this about?' he said, quickly changing the subject and looking around the room.

'I got Horace to agree to weddings at Bamton Hall,' blurted Amber.

She could kick herself. As usual, all the pretty words she'd planned - about showing him how she really felt, about saying sorry, about wanting to stay here at Bamton Hall with him - deserted her. It was like describing their first kiss all over again - where she missed out all the magic and just blurted out the obvious.

'You did?!' said Will, his face lighting up.

Amber nodded. 'I'm not good with words. I get stuck and tongue-tied. And - like you said before - Horace couldn't *see* it . . . so I decided to show him. It wasn't just me - Emmy roped in the rest of the book club girls, plus Mia and the kids . . .'

'It looks amazing,' he said, finally approaching her, his eyes on the flowers in the arch overhead. 'Even better than I imagined.'

Amber nodded.

'Will-' she took a deep breath as he came to stand right next to her, looking down into her eyes. 'I had so much I wanted to say to you - and now I've just messed it all up and I can't get it out and . . .' she trailed off as a lump of emotion got caught in her throat.

Will reached out and took one of her hands in his, running his thumb slowly over the back of it.

'So,' he said quietly, 'stop trying to tell me.' He looked around at the room again and a huge smile spread across his face. 'You've already shown me how you feel.'

Amber reached out and took his other hand. Lacing her fingers through his, she raised herself up until their lips met in the softest kiss.

Just like last time, the entire world seemed to pause as the warmth of his lips on hers spread through her body, melting everything else away.

'You know,' said Will, gently pulling back from her for a second, 'it's just not the same without a hosepipe.'

CHAPTER 16

'Willllllll?'

Amber watched as Belle tugged at Will's trouser leg, doing her best not to laugh. There was no doubt about it, that little monkey was definitely her biggest competition for Will's affection . . . not that she minded in the slightest. The sight of him gathering Belle up in his arms so that she could see over the fence to watch Richie zooming in and out of the hay bales on his Go-Kart was enough to melt her heart.

'Better?' he asked as Belle wrapped her arms around his neck.

'Only if you make pizza later?'

'Not later, Belly,' said Amber, 'but you're coming up for another princess sleepover next week, remember?'

Belle nodded and then started cheering as Richie zoomed close to them. 'Can we go see Alf next? I wanna cuddle Thor!'

'Don't you want to finish watching Richie first?' said Amber, her heart leaping with an excited fizz as Will reached over and caught hold of her hand.

'Nope,' said Belle. 'He's gonna be aaaaages, and mum and dad are watching anyway!'

Will grinned at Amber. 'The princess has a point. I think it's time to check everyone's alright anyway.'

'Come on then,' said Amber with a grin. 'I'll just go and tell Mia what we're up to,' she said quietly to Will. 'Catch up in a second?'

Will nodded. 'Come on Belle, we'll go and find that horse and then see what everyone else is up to, shall we?'

'Yeah! And a burger!'

'Another one?' said Will.

Amber watched as they wandered off together, the pair of them chatting away like old friends.

'You lost your man already?' laughed Ben as Amber drew near to the straw bale they were perched on.

She shrugged, grinning. 'Afraid his heart belongs to your little princess!'

'We can take her off your hands if you'd like some peace and quiet together?' said Mia.

'Are you kidding? They're having a ball!'

'As long as you're sure.'

'Of course. I just wanted to let you know that we're off to see Thor and Alf, and I wouldn't be surprised if a little cart trip might be in the offing at some point . . . if only to distract Belle from the idea of burger number three!'

'Ha! At least she hasn't got Will baking a special pizza for her yet,' laughed Ben, 'it's all she's asked for ever since she came to stay with you guys.'

'Don't you believe it,' chuckled Amber, 'she's already put her order in for pizza at princess party mark two.'

'Little monkey,' said Mia with a proud grin.

∼

After waving over to Richie, Amber left Mia and Ben cuddled up on their straw bale and set off across the paddock towards the rest of the fayre, which was in full swing. She couldn't believe how lucky they'd been. It was one of those beautiful autumn days, as soft and golden as a ripe apple, showing off Bamton Hall at its very best.

Every single one of the stalls was busy, and the two little workshops she'd already run at her joint stall with Emmy had been packed - everyone keen to make the little woven hearts and stars she'd chosen for the projects.

She wandered over towards the hook-a-duck stall that Horace had decided to set up at the last minute, and paused to watch three little kids struggling with their wooden poles, chasing the wayward plastic ducks around their paddling pool with much giggling.

All three were in full costume, ready for the parade

that was coming up in a few minutes. It really was quite something to see an angel, a devil and a pumpkin battling it out over the same plastic duck!

'How are you doing, my girl?' asked Horace, coming over to stand with her a moment.

'Wonderful,' beamed Amber. 'You?'

'Likewise,' nodded Horace with a contented look on his face. 'This,' he said, looking around at the crowded lawn full of locals who were all drinking, eating and laughing together, 'this is my idea of heaven.'

'Good!' said Amber, grinning at him. 'You deserve it!'

'And it was a great idea to announce our plans for the West Wing earlier - so many people have been through to have a look at the library. I must thank Emmy for freshening up the flowers - it looks absolutely glorious in there today!'

'She's knee-deep in customers at the moment, by the looks of things,' laughed Amber, peeping over at the stall. 'She'll be sold out before we know it!'

'Marvellous,' said Horace. 'I think we'll have made a nice chunk of change for the Church Fund by the end of today, don't you?'

Amber nodded. 'And for the hall too, I hope.'

'I can't believe how generous people have been,' said Horace, shaking his head.

Amber shrugged. 'This is Little Bamton. They love the hall, and they love you.'

'So it seems,' said Horace, and Amber was alarmed

to see tears pool in the corners of his eyes. He quickly took a red and white spotted hanky out of his pocket and dabbed at them.

'Are you okay?' said Violet, appearing at his side.

'More than okay, dear,' he said, giving a sniff. 'I'm just about perfect.'

'Oh good,' said Violet, patting him on the elbow, 'because I think you might be needed over at the WI stand. The terrible two are back with a vengeance, it seems!'

Amber and Horace both spun around in time to see Diesel and Tarmac, both dressed in giant-tarantula costumes in honour of the occasion, causing absolute havoc. Violet, however, was too late with her warning. The dogs had managed to pilfer a scone apiece and were now gleefully scampering towards the bouncy-castle with their spoils, all sixteen fake, fuzzy legs wiggling as they went.

Horace shrugged. 'Disaster averted,' he said.

'Hardly!' scoffed Violet, as shrieks emanated from the bouncy castle.

'I'm sure it'll be fine,' he grinned. 'Anyway Amber, where's Will? There's something I wanted to tell you both.'

'I'm right here!' said Will, appearing from the crowd.

'Me too!' said Belle at his side. 'Did you see the naughty doggies? Oooooh, can I have a go?' she asked, eyeballing the hook-a-duck.

'Let's get you a hook,' said Violet, taking her hand and leading her over to the pool.

'What did you want to tell us?' said Will, casually draping his arm around Amber's waist and making her shiver with delight.

'Well,' said Horace with a grin, 'I need you to get on and speak to the council tomorrow about our wedding venue licence.'

'Wow, okay,' said Will, looking surprised. 'I'm really glad you're keen - but . . . why the rush?'

'Well,' said Horace beaming, 'I've just taken our first ever booking!'

'You haven't?!' said Amber with a squeal.

'Certainly have. As long as we can get it all sorted out in time . . .'

'This is amazing!' said Will. 'When for?'

'The day before Christmas Eve,' said Horace.

Will thought about it for a second and nodded. 'That's enough time. Just.' He grinned at Horace. 'This is incredible news, congratulations,' he said, clapping Horace on the arm.

'Well, it's thanks to you,' said Horace. 'Both of you!'

Will drew Amber close to him and kissed her cheek, making her blush.

'So,' she said, wriggling slightly, 'who's it for?'

'Us,' came a gentle voice from behind them.

Will and Amber both twisted around to come face to face with Lucy and Sue.

'You?' gasped Amber, 'Oh my-'! She flew at the pair

of them, wrapping her arms Sue first and then hoiking Lucy into the mix, all three of them jumping up and down in excitement.

It was several minutes before they broke apart, giggling.

'You're invited of course!' laughed Sue.

'Can I have a plus-one?' said Amber.

Sue raised her eyebrows and glanced over at Will. 'Only if you promise to choose carefully!' she said, winking.

Amber, turned and took both of Will's hands in her own, lacing their fingers together as she smiled up at him.

'I promise.'

THE END

ALSO BY BETH RAIN

Little Bamton Series:

Little Bamton: The Complete Series Collection: Books 1 - 5

Individual titles:

Christmas Lights and Snowball Fights (Little Bamton Book 1)

Spring Flowers and April Showers (Little Bamton Book 2)

Summer Nights and Pillow Fights (Little Bamton Book 3)

Autumn Cuddles and Muddy Puddles (Little Bamton Book 4)

Christmas Flings and Wedding Rings (Little Bamton Book 5)

Upper Bamton Series:

A New Arrival in Upper Bamton (Upper Bamton Book 1)

Rainy Days in Upper Bamton (Upper Bamton Book 2)

Hidden Treasures in Upper Bamton (Upper Bamton Book 3)

Time Flies By in Upper Bamton (Upper Bamton Book 4)

Standalone Books:

Christmas on Crumcarey

Seabury Series:

Welcome to Seabury (Seabury Book 1)

Trouble in Seabury (Seabury Book 2)

Christmas in Seabury (Seabury Book 3)

Sandwiches in Seabury (Seabury Book 4)

Secrets in Seabury (Seabury Book 5)

Surprises in Seabury (Seabury Book 6)

Dreams and Ice Creams in Seabury (Seabury Book 7)

Mistakes and Heartbreaks in Seabury (Seabury Book 8)

Laughter and Happy Ever After in Seabury (Seabury Book 9)

Seabury Series Collections:

Kate's Story: Books 1 - 3

Hattie's Story: Books 4 - 6

Writing as Bea Fox:

What's a Girl To Do? The Complete Series

Individual titles:

The Holiday: What's a Girl To Do? (Book 1)

The Wedding: What's a Girl To Do? (Book 2)

The Lookalike: What's a Girl To Do? (Book 3)

The Reunion: What's a Girl To Do? (Book 4)

At Christmas: What's a Girl To Do? (Book 5)

ABOUT THE AUTHOR

Beth Rain has always wanted to be a writer and has been penning adventures for characters ever since she learned to stare into the middle-distance and daydream.

She currently lives in the (sometimes) sunny South West, and it is a dream come true to spend her days hanging out with Bob – her trusty laptop – scoffing crisps and chocolate while dreaming up swoony love stories for all her imaginary friends.

Beth's writing will always deliver on the happy-ever-afters, so if you need cosy… you're in safe hands!

Visit www.bethrain.com for all the bookish goodness and keep up with all Beth's news by joining her monthly newsletter!

        facebook.com/BethRainBooks
        twitter.com/bethrainauthor
        instagram.com/bethrainauthor

Printed in Great Britain
by Amazon